In the distance W▊ ▊ ▊ a tall male stridi▊▊ ▊ path, and her hea▊▊ ▊ though she'd received a shock while breathing suddenly became a distinct challenge. Perspiration beaded her upper lip, heat washing over her as she recalled what an absolute idiot she had been two years earlier…falling for her boss, *sleeping* with her boss.

Eros paused, all sleek, lithe and sexy elegance in a charcoal-gray suit and overcoat, a red silk scarf bright at his throat as he stood scanning the playground with the raw self-assurance of a highly successful tycoon.

His brilliant gaze settled on her and she went even stiffer, turning her head away to check on Teddy.

Teddy zoomed down the slide with a whoop, clambered off at the bottom and raced around to repeat the exercise.

"Why didn't you tell me about him?" Eros breathed soft and low and deadly.

Billionaires at the Altar

The world's wealthiest men...redeemed by their innocent brides!

Stamboulas Fotakis will stop at *nothing* to protect his three granddaughters. So, with their reputations in jeopardy, he decides to play matchmaker. Soon, the Mardas sisters find three unexpected billionaires at their doorstep—and they've each brought a diamond ring!

But convincing Winnie, Vivi and Zoe to be their convenient brides isn't going to be easy... If they're to walk down the aisle, then these billionaires must prove that their marriages are more than just business deals. Can the burning intensity of their wedding nights begin to melt the hearts of the world's wealthiest men?

Find out what happens in:

Winnie and Eros's story

The Greek Claims His Shock Heir

Available now!

Vivi and Raffaele's story

Zoe and Raj's story

Coming soon!

Lynne Graham

THE GREEK CLAIMS HIS SHOCK HEIR

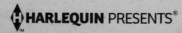

HARLEQUIN PRESENTS®

Recycling programs
for this product may
not exist in your area.

ISBN-13: 978-1-335-47801-6

The Greek Claims His Shock Heir

First North American publication 2019

Printed in U.S.A.

www.Harlequin.com

Lynne Graham was born in Northern Ireland and has been a keen romance reader since her teens. She is very happily married to an understanding husband who has learned to cook since she started to write! Her five children keep her on her toes. She has a very large dog who knocks everything over, a very small terrier who barks a lot and two cats. When time allows, Lynne is a keen gardener.

Books by Lynne Graham

Harlequin Presents

The Italian's Inherited Mistress

Wedlocked!

Claimed for the Leonelli Legacy
His Queen by Desert Decree

Brides for the Taking

The Desert King's Blackmailed Bride
The Italian's One-Night Baby
Sold for the Greek's Heir

Vows for Billionaires

The Secret Valtinos Baby
Castiglione's Pregnant Princess
Da Rocha's Convenient Heir

Visit the Author Profile page
at Harlequin.com for more titles.

PROLOGUE

STAMBOULAS FOTAKIS, KNOWN as Bull—but only behind his back, because nobody wanted to offend one of the richest men in the world—studied the new photograph on his desk. It featured his three granddaughters and his great-grandson, none of whom he had even known existed until a few weeks earlier. His competitors would have been shocked by the softness of the older man's gaze as he looked with pride and satisfaction at his only living relatives. Three beautiful girls and a handsome little boy...

At the same time—and it had to be faced—those three girls' lives and that little boy's life were in an almighty mess, Stam acknowledged with bristling annoyance. If *only* he had known they were out there, orphaned and growing up in state care, *he* would've given them a home and raised them. Sadly, he had not been given that choice and his granddaughters had suffered accordingly. But he didn't blame *them* for their chaotic lives, he blamed himself for throwing his youngest son, Cy, out of the family for defying him. Of course, twenty-odd years ago, Stam had been a very different man, he conceded wryly, an impatient, autocratic and inflexible man. Possibly, he had learned a thing or two since then. His late wife had never forgiven him for disowning Cy. In the end, all of them had paid too high a price for Stam's act of idiocy.

But that was then and this was *now*, Stam reminded himself, and it was time he sorted out his granddaughters' lives. He would begin by righting the wrongs done to his new family members. He had the power and the wealth to do that and for that reality he was grateful. He wasn't seeking revenge, he assured himself assiduously, he would only be doing what was best for his grandchildren. First he would sort out Winnie, tiny dark-eyed Winnie, who bore such a very strong resemblance to Stam's late wife, an Arabian princess called Azra.

At least Winnie already spoke a little Greek, only a handful of words admittedly, but that was a promising start. Her problems would be the most easily solved, he reasoned, although how he would hold on to his temper and deal civilly with the adulterous cheat who had made Winnie a mistress and Stam's grandson a bastard, he didn't yet know, for Eros Nevrakis was an infuriatingly powerful man in his own right.

CHAPTER ONE

'Mr Fotakis will be free in just a few minutes,' the PA informed Eros Nevrakis as he stood at the window overlooking the bay while she regarded him with far more appreciation than the magnificent view could ever have roused in her. He was a tall, broad-shouldered man in his early thirties, and his legendary good looks had not been exaggerated, the young woman conceded admiringly. He had a shock of black glossy curls and brilliant green eyes that more than one appreciative woman had been heard to compare to emeralds.

The view from the small island of Trilis would not be half as impressive as that from Bull Fotakis's private estate, Eros was thinking with rueful amusement. On this particular morning Eros was in the very best of moods. After all, he had made several offers through intermediaries to buy back Trilis from Stam Fotakis and those offers had been royally ignored. That he had finally been awarded a meeting with the reclusive old curmudgeon was a very healthy hint that Bull was finally willing to sell the island back to Eros.

Trilis, however, was greener and rather less developed than the extensive estate that Fotakis owned outside Athens and maintained as his headquarters, complete with office blocks and employees on-site. Of course, Fotakis had always been a famous workaholic. When Eros's father had gone bust in the nineties and had been forced into selling his family home, everyone had assumed that Fotakis was planning to build a new base on the private island, only that hadn't happened. Should he ever contrive to regain ownership of the island, Eros planned to open an upmarket resort on the coast that would generate jobs and rejuvenate the local economy. The old man, however, had done nothing with Trilis but hadn't seemed interested in selling it either.

So, what had changed? Eros ruminated, irritated that he was unable to answer that question. He preferred to know what motivated his competitors and opponents because ignorance of such revealing details was always risky. Going in blind wasn't smart, especially when Fotakis was too rich to be tempted by money. Eros turned the question around, considering it shrewdly from another angle. What did *he* currently *have* that Fotakis *wanted*? Eros asked himself then, reckoning that that was likely to be a far more accurate reading of the situation. Bull Fotakis was notoriously crafty and devious.

At the same time, Eros was uncomfortably aware that he would pay just about any price to regain the island of Trilis because it was the sole possession his father had truly regretted losing.

'It is our *family* place and if you lose family, you lose everything. I learned that the hard way,' his father had rasped painfully on his deathbed. 'Promise me that if you do well in the future, you'll do everything you can to buy Trilis back. It's the Nevrakis home and your ancestors and mine are buried there.'

Eros compressed his sensual mouth, shying away from such sentimental recollections from the past. He had learned from his father's mistakes. A man had to be *hard* in business and in his private life, not soft, not easily led or seduced. And a man forced to deal with a Greek icon of achievement like Bull Fotakis had to be even tougher.

'Mr Fotakis will see you now…'

Stam's gaze was hard when it zeroed in on Eros Nevrakis. A good-looking louse, he conceded grudgingly, exactly the type calculated to turn a young and naive woman's head. Nevrakis hadn't *told* Winnie that he was married. Stam had drilled every relevant fact out of his reluctant granddaughter. He had recognised her shame, gasping in relief that, despite his initial troubling assumptions about her character, her morals *were* in the right place. Winnie would *never* have knowingly slept with another woman's husband. Nevrakis had lied to her, conning her into a demeaning living arrangement before hanging her out to dry without a single regret.

Eros saw a small stocky bearded man with eyes as sharp as tacks set in a weathered face. His hair and his neat little beard were white as snow but there was no suggestion of Santa Claus about him. Eros took a seat and refused refreshment, keen to get down to business once the usual pleasantries had been aired.

'You want Trilis back,' Stam remarked, startling Eros with that candid opening and the complete lack of any social chit-chat. 'But *I* want something else.'

Eros leant back in his chair, long powerful legs carefully relaxed in pose. 'I assumed as much,' he quipped.

'I believe that you're divorced now.'

So random did that remark seem that Eros was disconcerted. He blinked, lashes longer than a girl's, Stam noted in disgust, while wondering simultaneously how he was going to tolerate the lying rat as a grandson-in-law. Unfortunately, little Teddy couldn't get his father's name without his mother also getting a wedding ring, so choice didn't come into it. Stam refused to stand back and allow his sole great-grandchild to remain illegitimate. He knew that was an old-fashioned outlook, but he didn't care because he hadn't got to the top of the ladder by bending his principles to suit other people's and he had no plans to change.

'I can't imagine why you would remark on that fact,' Eros drawled softly. 'But it is true. I was divorced last year.'

Stam gritted his teeth. 'Was that because you were thinking of marrying your mistress?'

'I have no idea where this strange conversation is heading,' Eros retorted crisply, lifting his strong chin in a challenging move of quiet strength. 'However, I can tell you that I've never had a mistress, but if I *did* have one, I seriously doubt that I would marry her.'

Stam went rigid with offence until he reminded himself that Nevrakis had no idea that he *could* be causing offence because he was not aware that Winnie was Stam's granddaughter and would undoubtedly never have dared to lay a single finger on her had he known that salient fact. He then chose to entertain himself by approaching his goal in a roundabout manner.

'My granddaughter is a single parent who needs a husband. That is my price for the island of Trilis. If you agree to marry her, no cash need change hands.'

Stunned by that bald assurance, Eros straightened

in his seat. 'You want me to *marry* your granddaughter?' he exclaimed, so taken aback by the idea that he could not even hide his consternation. 'I didn't know you had one. I'm sure I read somewhere that you had no relatives left alive…'

'Until recently, I thought that too,' Stam admitted equably. 'But then, surprises are the joy of life, don't you think?'

Still in the dark as to why Bull Fotakis should offer him such a staggering proposition, Eros could only think that he had always hated surprises. Surprises had, after all, marked some of the worst moments of his life since childhood, starting with the one when his father had killed Christmas by dropping in with his youthful girlfriend on his arm to announce that he was divorcing Eros's mother for making *him* feel old. Eros might have been only eight years of age at the time, but he had been old enough to feel every ounce of his mother's agonised pain and humiliation that the man she loved had fallen out of love with her. That experience had given him an inbuilt hatred of broken marriages and divorce, most especially because he could date the origins of his father's financial downfall from that same moment.

'I'm not sure I agree,' Eros sidestepped quietly. 'I'm certain you could offer your granddaughter to any one of a dozen wealthy, successful men and create an enthusiastic stampede… Why me?'

'You're not a fool,' Stam conceded, his weathered face grim at that grudging acknowledgement because he wasn't sure he *wanted* a grandson-in-law strong enough to stand up to him.

'I hope not,' Eros said in a calmer tone, but his brain was working at supersonic speed in an effort to work out the mystery of Fotakis's interest in him as a potential grandson-in-law. 'A single parent, you said…' he added, playing for time.

'*Ne*… Yes, a handsome little boy, *my* great-grandson.' Stam could not hide the possessive note in his voice or the pride because both his sons were dead and the sight of that little boy had softened his tough old heart. 'He needs a father figure, for who can tell how many years I have left?'

'You seem hale and hearty to me,' Eros murmured drily. 'But you still haven't explained why you have chosen me for this role.'

'And you still haven't explained how much you're willing to sacrifice to regain that island,' Stam countered smoothly. 'But I can assure you that if you fail to marry my granddaughter, I will ensure that you *never* reclaim Trilis.'

'Then we would appear to have reached the end of our meeting,' Eros retorted levelly, vaulting upright with the fluid grace of an athlete. 'I have no desire to remarry, and while I would *like* to reclaim Trilis, the loss of my freedom would be too high a price to pay.'

Stam loosed a sardonic laugh. 'Even if my great-grandson is also...*your son*?'

Those two words halted Eros in his tracks. His handsome dark head turned back, an expression of sheer incredulity etched in his lean bronzed features. 'Impossible!' he grated. 'I have no children!'

Stam surveyed him with loathing, as yet unconvinced that Eros was entirely unaware that Winnie had been pregnant when she had left his country house. 'Two more words: Winnie Mardas... Of course, you may not remember her?'

'Winnie?' Eros Nevrakis echoed in raw disbelief. 'She's *your* granddaughter?'

'Surprise...surprise,' Stam said meanly.

Eros hovered, his big powerful physique screaming with tension and scantily leashed energy. 'And you say...she has had *my* child? *My* son?'

'I do,' Stam confirmed. 'Of course, you're fully able to carry out your own DNA testing if you so wish. That's your business. All I care about is that you marry her without telling her that I interfered. Is that clear?'

Nothing was clear to Eros in that moment. He was in a severe state of shock laced with outrage. Two years back when he had last seen her, Winnie hadn't told him that she was pregnant, hadn't even hinted at such a possibility. She had just walked out of his life and never got back in touch. He was instantaneously enraged and equally appalled. A man had a *right* to know that he was a father, didn't he? The days when a man was routinely left in ignorance of paternity were long gone. These days a man's importance in the parenting stakes was supposed to be valued and acknowledged. Eros knew that the first person he would be consulting would be a lawyer.

'Eros…' Stam prompted. 'Did you hear what I said?'

'Is she *here*? Is she in Greece?' Eros demanded wrathfully.

'Sadly not, she's still in London living with her sisters. I can give you the address.'

'Please do.' Eros's clipped tone denoted savage impatience.

'You are not to tell her that *I* gave you the address,' Stam warned him as he tossed him a piece of paper already prepared with the relevant details. 'You do not tell her that you have met me and discussed her personal affairs.'

'You like to be the ringmaster without the applause?' Eros said derisively. 'Not sure I can deliver that.'

For all his seventy-odd years, Stam reared out of his chair like a coiled spring bouncing back into shape. 'If you let out one *word* of my role in this mess, I will destroy you!' he raked back at the younger man in threat. 'And you *know* I can do it!'

'But you don't know *me*,' Eros tossed back with perfect indifference to how Stam Fotakis felt about anything he did. He reckoned that Bull Fotakis could do many things to make business more challenging, but Eros was a billionaire in his own right with equally powerful friends and he was confident that the older man could *not* destroy him.

Stam dealt him a crushing appraisal in retribution for his disrespect. 'A married man taking one of his domestic staff to bed? I understand you perfectly. You picked her because she was poor and powerless and unlikely to be indiscreet for fear of dismissal. You made her your mistress and shifted her down to your country house for sleazy weekends. Be assured that I know exactly what kind of a man you are! A cheating, manipulative bastard!'

Eros flung back his handsome head, black curls tumbling back from his brilliant green eyes. 'And yet you want me to *marry* Winnie?'

'I want my great-grandson legitimised,' Stam ground out with finality. 'You get your precious island back. I don't expect you to live with Winnie or stay with her. In fact, I don't want you to because she could do a hell of a lot better than you as a husband and that little boy will have me as a male role model! He doesn't *need* you!'

Vexed way beyond the limit of expressing his explosive emotions, Eros swung on his heel and walked out, his wide shoulders and long back

rigid while he mentally rained down the hellfire
of revenge on Winnie and her offensive grandfather. How dared they?

How dared they?

Talk and behave as though he were powerless?
Dismiss his rights as a father as though they did
not exist? Suggest he could have no value as a parent? That, indeed, he would be a negative influence on his own child? They would pay for those
slurs, one way or another they would *both* pay,
Eros swore with inner vehemence.

Even worse, the implication that he was the sort
of man who preyed on his domestic staff like some
shady creep! Winnie had never been his mistress.
Eros had never had one and certainly not during his
marriage to Tasha. He had been celibate for years
and then Winnie had appeared and *somehow*... His
teeth gritted as he thrust the memory away, along
with all his other memories of Winnie Mardas. The
affair had been a mistake, a very human mistake
but still a mistake. He knew that very well. Temptation had led to an error and then ultimately to
freedom, he reminded himself, shelving that train
of thought for something much more important.

He had a child... He had a *son*, whose name he
didn't even know! Engaged in frantic mathemati-
cal calculations, Eros worked out that his little boy
had to be under two years of age, a mere toddler.
A faint shard of relief touched him. That wasn't

too late for a child to meet his father for the first time. How much worse would it have been if he had *never* found out or if the child had been much older and embittered by his father's long absence from his life?

Yeah, it could have been worse, he jeered at himself for such ruminations. But not much worse... Stam Fotakis threatening him, trying to stampede him into marriage when he had only just escaped an imprudent marriage, his first child estranged from him, the mother of his child equally estranged and her subsequent behaviour were inexcusable. Seriously, how *could* the situation have been worse?

And the whole chaotic fiasco stemmed from one mistake. Eros's own mistake, he acknowledged grudgingly. He had naively agreed to marry a young woman he didn't love and didn't desire to soothe a dying man's fears about his daughter's future. But it had never been a real marriage. He had never shared a bed with Tasha, had never even shared a home with her. Throughout their marriage they had lived entirely separate lives. He had accepted all the restrictions of marriage without receiving any of the benefits. And then Winnie had come into his life and logic, honour and restraint had gone out of the window simultaneously.

Stam Fotakis surveyed his empty office with bemused eyes. For the first time in his life, he wasn't sure how a business meeting had gone. It *had* been business, *purely* business, he told himself soothingly. But Nevrakis had gone up like a firework display, far more volatile in nature than Stam's careful research had led him to expect. He had never seen a man in such a rage, particularly not one renowned for being cooler than ice. Suppose he let that rage out in little Winnie's direction?

A new fear assailed Stam as he grabbed the phone to speak to his granddaughters' bodyguards, the security detail the girls didn't even know they had watching their every move in London. Possibly, security would have to be a little more visible in the near future, Stam reasoned worriedly. Nevrakis had left his office in violent haste…

'So,' Vivi summed up, copper hair as sleek as a swathe of silk framing her vivid face as she looked across the kitchen table at her sisters. 'Our grandfather is as crazy as a loon. Where does that leave us?'

'What we do is our choice.' Winnie threw back her head so that her mass of brunette hair tumbled down her back, enabling her to gather it up and expertly twist it into a ponytail, ready for work. 'Nobody can *force* us to do anything.'

'Agreed, but Grandad *is* our only option for the money we need,' Zoe piped up with innate practicality. 'Nobody else is willing to give us money to save John and Liz's home. We tried to get a loan and we failed.'

That unwelcome reminder fell like a brick into the tense silence.

Winnie tugged her little boy up onto her lap because he was drooping tiredly by her side. Teddy closed his eyes and relaxed, his little face drowsy below his crown of black curls. Talk was cheap and easy, but reality had just spoken in Zoe's quiet little voice, Winnie reflected ruefully. In truth, none of the three sisters had an actual choice. In the kindest way possible for a very rich tyrant, Stam Fotakis had spelt out the truth that his assistance would be given and gladly, but that financial help would come at a price they might not be prepared to pay.

And why did they need that financial help?

Their foster parents, John and Liz Brooke, whose care had transformed the sisters' lives and reunited them as a family group, were in deep financial trouble. When Winnie had learned that John and Liz were within days of having their ramshackle farmhouse repossessed and losing the foster children currently in their care, she had disregarded her long-dead father's warning and had approached her wealthy grandfather with a begging letter.

Stam Fotakis had cut off their late father, Cy, without a penny when he was barely more than a teenager. Cy had demonstrated his disdain for the family name by legally changing it to his grandmother's maiden name of Mardas, which, of course, had meant that their grandfather had had no way of tracing either his son or the family he had eventually had.

At twenty-six, Winnie was old enough to remember their parents, who had died in a car crash when she was eight, but Vivi had only the barest recollection of them, and Zoe, a mere toddler at the time, had none at all.

But all three young women were very much aware that the Brooke family had saved them when they'd needed saving, giving them the care and support they had long lacked to rise above the tragic loss of their mum and dad and the disturbing consequences that had followed because they had all had bad experiences in state care. Winnie, extracted from a physically abusive foster home, had arrived with them first, and John and Liz's caring enquiries and persistence had eventually led to the sisters being reunited within their home.

From that point on all their lives had improved beyond all recognition and gradually a happy, secure normality had enveloped the traumatised siblings. You couldn't put a price on what John and Liz had done for them, Winnie conceded ruefully, because you couldn't put a price on love. Without adopting them, John and Liz had become the girls' forever family, treating them like daughters and encouraging and supporting them every step of the way into adulthood.

'That's true.' Vivi spoke up again with a grimace at the reminder that they had failed to get a loan. 'And we can only get that money if we agree to marry men hand-picked by our crazy grandad. Obviously getting his granddaughters married off to suitable men is hugely important to him.'

'He did say they didn't have to be *real* marriages… in-name-only stuff is rather different,' Winnie muttered the reminder ruefully, because in truth she didn't want to get married either, even if it did only mean a piece of legal paper and a ring on her finger.

When she had first contacted her grandfather, she had had to provide documents to prove her identity but, barely a week later, she and her sisters and her little boy had been flown out on a private jet to Greece for several days. They had been stunned by their grandfather's wealth and his very big and opulent home and had been well on the road to liking him *until* he had mentioned his terms for giving them the money to save the roof over John's and Liz's heads.

Of the three of them, Winnie had been most shocked by those terms, particularly when it should've been obvious to a man who had bitterly lamented their unhappy childhood in foster care that *he* too owed John and Liz Brooke a moral debt for the care they had taken of his grandchildren. But evidently the concept of giving something for nothing was not one Stam Fotakis was willing to embrace. Yes, he had acknowledged he was delighted to learn of their existence and very grateful that John and Liz had given them such wonderful care…but still he had had to mention *terms*…

Winnie had immediately scolded herself for her sentimental expectations and unrealistic hopes of her grandfather. He was the same man who had thrown his younger son out of his home for refusing to study business at university and he had never looked back from that hard decision. Not necessarily a kind man, not even necessarily a *nice* man. He wanted them all married off to what he had referred to as 'men of substance' and restored to the society position he saw as their Fotakis birthright. Winnie, however, did suspect that she knew *why* Stam Fotakis had decided not to simply invite his grandchildren into his home to gift them that birthright as members of his household.

Stam Fotakis was *ashamed* of his granddaughters' current status. He had adored her son, Teddy, on sight but had been appalled that Winnie was unmarried. He had been equally shocked by the dreadful scandal in which Vivi had become innocently embroiled. In fact, Stam Fotakis didn't have a modern laid-back bone in his entire body.

He believed women should be safely, decently married before they had children and that their names should only ever appear in a downmarket tabloid newspaper because they were beautifully dressed VIPs.

Winnie grimaced. She had always believed that she too would be married before she had a child but a crueller fate had tripped her up and she was a little wiser now. Falling in love with the wrong man could be a disaster and that was the crux of what had happened to Winnie and her once-fine ideals. Her only consolation was that she had not once suspected that Eros was a married man, and he had most definitely concealed that reality from her. Her wake-up call had come in the shape of a visit from Eros's wife, Tasha, and she still broke out in a cold sweat just remembering that awful day. It had forced her to grow up fast though, she told herself bracingly, and she had needed that 'short sharp shock' treatment to get the strength to walk away from the man she loved.

'I have to get ready for work.' Winnie sighed, rising from her seat.

Zoe stood up, as well. 'Give me Teddy,' she urged. 'I'll put him down for a nap while I make dinner and that'll allow you to slip out without him noticing.'

Zoe was tiny like Winnie but her hair was golden blonde as their father's had been. Her grandfather had told Winnie that she bore a close resemblance to her grandmother who had apparently been an Arabian princess. Winnie shook her head over that startling recollection because nothing could have more surely pointed out that her grandfather came from a very different world. Her father, Cy, had never once mentioned his mother's exalted birth, but he had talked very lovingly about her.

Smiling at her youngest sibling, Winnie recognised how very lucky she was to have sisters who loved and cared for her son as much as she did. She could never have managed without them although the fact that, as a junior chef, she invariably worked evenings and weekends helped in the childcare department. They had also been living in a dump of a flat before they met their grandfather and Winnie had only accepted the older man's generous offer of new accommodation for her son's sake. In the space of two weeks, however, that new comfortable terraced home with its four generous bedrooms and extra space, not to mention its smart location, had changed their lives very much for the better. They weren't paying rent any more either, which meant that surviving on their low salaries was no longer a struggle.

Even so, it didn't feel safe to be depending even temporarily on the generosity of a grandfather who was very much a mixed bag of traits and tricks. Winnie was painfully aware that Stam Fotakis could decide to turn his back on them as quickly as he had laid down a welcome mat for them. Rich people, she had learned from her experience with Eros Nevrakis, could be unreliable and volatile. It didn't do to trust them or to expect them to stay the same like more ordinary folk, she recalled sickly.

'I'm sorry, I'm not in the mood tonight.' She recalled Eros murmuring in apology, as if it were perfectly normal to push her away when he was usually keen to encourage her affection. That rejection had hurt, it had hurt *so much*, acting on her like the very first frightening wake-up call to reality.

Her eyes stinging, Winnie compressed her lips and shut down the memory fast. Remembering Eros was a two-edged sword that both wounded *and* infuriated her. She had been so stupidly naive and trusting, refusing to see or suspect what her grandfather had picked up instantly…that she had not been engaged in a passionate love affair but had instead become a married man's mistress. And there was nothing remotely romantic or loving or caring about that role, she concluded as she stepped onto the Tube to travel to the restaurant that currently employed her as a pastry chef. She would've been rather higher up the career ladder had she not dropped out of her apprenticeship to become Eros Nevrakis's personal chef, she reflected resentfully. On the other hand, she would never have had Teddy without *him* and, no matter what her grandfather thought of unmarried mothers, Teddy could never ever be a source of regret.

Midevening, Vivi was just tucking the little boy into his jammies when a loud knock sounded on the front door. The knocker sounded again before she even reached the hall with Teddy clutched precariously below one arm, because you couldn't turn your back safely on Teddy for even ten seconds. 'All right…all right…try being patient,' she was muttering below her breath as she yanked open the door and gaped.

At least five men stood on the doorstep, all big, all wearing dark suits and earphones. No, the one standing closest wasn't wearing one of those communication things and he looked madder than fire.

'Are you okay, Miss Mardas?' one of the men at the back enquired.

'Who on earth are you all?' Vivi whispered, feeling unusually intimidated.

'Security, Miss Mardas. We work for your grandfather.'

'I'm not security,' Eros spelt out impatiently while trying not to squint to get a better look at the little boy anchored sideways below the redhead's arm. His brain went momentarily blank as he focused on that grinning, lively little face below the splash of black curls. His son, assuming it was his son, looked very much like him, Eros acknowledged, momentarily shocked out of the rage that had powered him all the way from Greece.

'Why would I need security?' Vivi whispered.

'I want to see Winnie,' Eros grated. 'I am Eros Nevrakis.'

Vivi froze and immediately awarded him a look of utter loathing. 'My sister is at work.'

'I will come in and wait for her, then.'

'She won't be home until after midnight, so there's no point in you waiting,' Vivi proclaimed with pursed lips.

Eros drew himself up to his full six feet four inches and simply looked through her, unperturbed by her hostile manner. 'I will return at ten in the morning. Tell her to ensure that she is here then,' he delivered through clenched white teeth.

CHAPTER TWO

'No—NO WAY am I seeing him after all this time,' Winnie declared wearily after her shift with both her sisters treating her to an anxious appraisal. 'What on earth does he want?'

'Do you think he's found out about Teddy?' Zoe piped up worriedly.

'I don't see how.'

'Grandad knows him,' Vivi interposed thoughtfully. 'I saw the look on his face when you admitted Teddy's father was Greek and when you finally gave him the guy's name, he was really, really furious—didn't you notice?'

'No, I wasn't wanting to look at Grandad while I was being forced to tell that particular story,' Winnie admitted, her face burning at that memory.

'Well, Nevrakis can't *force* you to see him. Go to the park as usual,' Vivi advised.

'Don't you think—with him being Teddy's father—that that is a bit unwise?' Zoe murmured, as always the peacemaker.

'He's *not* Teddy's father. He's never been here for Teddy *or* Winnie when they needed him!' Vivi sharply snapped back at Zoe.

'It's just I think…well, you know…er…that fathers have rights,' Zoe said hesitantly. 'And maybe if he knows about Teddy and that's why he's here, if you don't play nice, he might start thinking about taking you to court to get permission to see him.'

'Dear heaven, I hope not!' Winnie gasped in horror but the more she thought about that risk, the more worrying the situation became. But was it really that likely that Eros would be that interested in a child?

Could Eros already know about Teddy? Could her grandfather have told him? She wouldn't have trusted Stam Fotakis as far as she could throw him. He had already told her that she should've informed Eros that she was pregnant rather than simply walking away from their relationship without an explanation. *For* walk, *substitute* run, she thought unhappily, for the discovery that Eros was a married man had devastated Winnie, and after that deception she hadn't felt she owed Eros the news that she was pregnant. She hadn't wanted anything more to do with him, hadn't ever wanted to even *see* him again…but now he had tracked her down and with Teddy around that was a game changer, wasn't it?

* * *

Clutching her hand, Teddy chattered non-stop all the way to the park. It was toddler chatter in which only one word in ten was recognisable as an actual word. They had to walk slowly too, because Teddy loved to walk. But he had short legs and if she lost patience and put him in the buggy, he would throw a tantrum. 'Not baby!' he would scream, mortally offended by such a demeaning mode of transport.

He gave a shout of excitement once he saw the playground, tearing free of his mother's grasp to race down the path in advance of her. Winnie broke into a run because Teddy's fearless approach to life often put him at risk. By the time she caught up, he was climbing the steps to the slide. He had been as agile as a little monkey from an early age. He whooped as he went down the slide and she retreated to a concrete bench nearby, relieved to sit down because she was still tired from the night before.

Her phone buzzed in her pocket and she dug it out.

It was Vivi.

'Nevrakis is coming to see you at the park,' her sibling warned her. 'I tried to put him off but he said he would stay and wait if I didn't tell him where you were.'

Near panic engulfed Winnie, her jaw dropping at the thought of being cornered by Eros in a public place. But he wasn't the type to make a scene, she reminded herself doggedly, and she couldn't avoid him for ever. It was better to be sensible, she told herself bracingly, smoothing down her warm jacket, wishing she had put on a little make-up, telling herself off furiously for even caring how she might look while her nerves rattled about inside her like jumping beans. He had to know about Teddy, had to want to see him because there was no other reason for him to seek her out now. Her mind wanted to take her back to her very first meeting with Eros Nevrakis but she wouldn't let it because memories would weaken her, tearing away the superficial calm she had learned to keep in place to make her sisters happy.

'Oh, sure, I'm over him!' she had taught herself to declare with a laugh for punctuation. 'I'm not stupid!'

Two men lodged nearby below the trees, suited and smart. Her grandfather's utterly superfluous bodyguards, whom Vivi had met the night before on the doorstep, Winnie suspected, and she ignored them. She would have to phone her grandfather about that unnecessary extravagance. Why on earth would she and her sisters need guarding when as yet nobody even knew they were related to Stam Fotakis?

In the distance she glimpsed a tall man striding down the path and her heart stuttered as though she'd received a shock, while breathing suddenly became a distinct challenge. Perspiration beaded her short upper lip, heat washing over her as she recalled what an absolute idiot she had been two years earlier...falling for her boss, *sleeping* with her boss.

Eros paused, all sleek, lithe and sexy elegance in a charcoal-grey suit and overcoat, a red silk scarf bright at his throat as he stood scanning the playground with the raw self-assurance of a highly successful tycoon. Winnie swallowed hard, her hands clenching together, nails biting into her tender palms. She had to force herself to stand upright to catch his attention because she wasn't going to hide from him and refused to behave as if she feared him.

His brilliant gaze settled on her and she went even stiffer, turning her head away to check on Teddy, standing at the top of the slide shouting for her attention, for if there was one thing Teddy loved it was an audience. He was an irredeemable little extrovert, brimming with vitality. She moved closer to the slide, ignoring Eros to the best of her ability, even as she heard his steps sound behind her.

Teddy zoomed down the slide with a whoop, clambered off at the bottom and raced round to repeat the exercise.

'Why didn't you tell me about him?' Eros breathed, soft and low and deadly.

Disconcertion turned Winnie's head in his direction and she saw him in profile because his entire attention was studiously welded to her son. That classic bronzed profile made her heart give a sick thud inside her chest and she swallowed hard, close enough to smell the rich aromatic scent of his designer cologne, close enough to be dragged down screaming into the kind of memories she always suppressed, and she took a hasty step backwards, protecting herself from getting too close.

'Why didn't you tell me that you were married?' Winnie parried quietly.

Eros gritted his even white teeth, incensed by that comeback. He turned to study her as involuntarily entranced by her tiny proportions as he had been the first time he saw her. She was a barely five-feet-tall brunette with delicate curves and a tiny waist, so small and light he could have scooped her up with one powerful hand. Of course, pregnancy could have changed her shape, he conceded, but he was challenged to picture Winnie pregnant and the loose jacket she wore concealed more than it revealed of her figure. The huge chocolate-brown eyes, sultry pink mouth and the lustrous dark mane of her hair, however, were unchanged. He tore his electrified gaze from her, angry enough to spit tacks, and concentrated his attention back on his son.

The little boy was definitely *his* son and he was of a much sturdier build than his mother. That tumble of black curls and those green eyes, the same green eyes that Eros had inherited from his late mother, unmistakeably marked Teddy out as a Nevrakis. Eros had done his homework and made his own enquiries since that meeting two days earlier with Stam Fotakis. His son was called Teddy. What sort of a name was that? His child had been named after a plush toy, he thought witheringly. But the biggest surprise of all for Eros at that moment was how looking at Teddy made him *feel*…

As though that little creature had been put on this earth purely for him to protect, he acknowledged in wonderment, watching as Teddy climbed the slide steps at speed and threw himself down it with dangerous enthusiasm and a noisy shout. Impelled by a response that bit too deep to withstand, Eros strode forward and swept the little boy upright again with careful hands. Teddy gave him a startled look and then a huge cheerful smile as Eros gently set him free again.

'Swing, Mama,' Teddy demanded, setting off in that direction.

'He's bossy like you,' Winnie said drily.

Eros ignored her. He had a great deal to say to Winnie but none of it could be safely voiced where they could be overheard.

Winnie lifted Teddy into one of the baby swings and gave him a push before standing back.

'How old is he?' Eros demanded in a driven undertone.

'Eighteen months. He's tall for his age,' Winnie muttered.

'And in all that time you didn't *once* think of contacting me?' Eros intoned through clenched teeth of restraint.

'You were married,' Winnie reminded him with a lift of her chin.

'That's irrelevant,' Eros countered with ferocious bite. 'It's not an excuse.'

'I'm not making excuses. I don't regret not telling you,' Winnie responded, outraged by his lack of guilt.

'But you will,' Eros murmured, soft as a cat padding round her on velvet paws of menace. 'You will *learn* to regret it.'

A faint chill stiffened Winnie's already rigid spine but she squared her slight shoulders, rebelling against that sense of threat. Eros couldn't push her around; he couldn't *do* anything to her. Teddy was hers and she didn't work for Eros any more or indeed depend on him in any way.

Her defiance infuriated Eros. Evidently he had underestimated Winnie when he had deemed her to be a quiet, restful sort of young woman; the type who would never cause waves in his life. He had trusted her as far as he trusted any woman, had believed he knew her inside out, had only registered how mistaken such an assumption could be after she had vanished into thin air. His wide sensual mouth compressed into a grim line.

Winnie glanced at him and her tension zoomed to a new high, her eyes lingering against her will on his lean, powerful length, her breath catching in her throat. With an effort she tore her attention away again but her senses were humming, her heart was pounding, teaching her that she had yet to attain the level of indifference she needed to be safe around him. Instead she was mesmerised by that stormy, striking male beauty of his, the honed, flawless angles of his high cheekbones, the definitive shape of his nose and the unforgettably stunning impact of those jewelled green eyes, once seen, never forgotten. She shifted her feet, fighting off her susceptibility, hating herself for noticing afresh just how gorgeous he was.

'My only regret is that I ever met you,' she declared stonily.

'A little late in the day,' Eros purred, impervious to the insult. 'I will take you to my apartment, where we will talk about where we go from here.'

'No,' Winnie argued. 'I'm going home. Teddy needs his nap.'

To Eros's mind, Teddy looked more as if he was good to go for another few hours as he gripped the swing and kicked up his legs with excitement.

'We can't talk with your sisters present,' Eros countered very drily.

'My sisters will have left for work.' Rigid with resentment that he was somehow contriving to force her into a discussion she didn't want as well as granting him access to her home, Winnie slung him a look of loathing, big brown eyes awash with annoyance.

She hated Eros Nevrakis. She had never hated anyone before but she hated him for a whole host of reasons. But she had to find out *what* he wanted, had to remember that he was Teddy's father and should for the present be handled with tact, she reminded herself quellingly. This time running away wasn't an option because she would only leave a bigger mess behind her. Her soft full lips compressed, she lifted her son out of the swing, ignoring his bitter wail of complaint. He looked up at her with green eyes swimming with tears and her heart clenched as she set him down to walk beside her.

'We'll use my limo,' Eros informed her.

'No, Teddy and I will walk back. I'll meet you there,' Winnie told him without hesitation and she turned on her heel, needing the time alone and the peace to regroup and calm down.

Teddy dragged his heels all the way, tired now and cross, but Winnie barely noticed because all the memories she had buried were flooding her to drowning point.

Fresh from catering college and a variety of jobs in which she'd picked up experience, she had secured a sous chef position in a small family-owned Greek restaurant. When a virus had put the head chef in bed, the responsibility for providing dinner for a large party of Greek businessmen being entertained by Eros had fallen on Winnie's shoulders. At the end of the meal she had been invited to meet the client, and she could still recall getting into a panic at the prospect and dragging off her chef's hat and tidying her hair for the sort of public appearance that had never come her way before.

Eros had complimented her with flattering enthusiasm on the meal she had prepared. She had hovered there with bright red cheeks, trying not to gawp at the best-looking man she had ever met, wondering how anyone could have such extraordinarily green eyes, intense as polished tourmalines in that lean, darkly handsome face of his. He had passed her his business card, telling her that he was looking for a personal chef for his London home and that when she was free she should ring him for an interview.

She had been quite happy where she was working, but she didn't see much of her sisters because she worked such awkward hours and that more than anything had persuaded her to make that phone call. When she had been offered a salary far beyond her current earnings and accommodation in central London to boot, she had accepted, reasoning that working as a billionaire's private chef would offer her even more exciting opportunities to advance herself. With two sisters who were still students, invariably broke and in need of clothes, the ability to earn a decent wage had been very important back then.

'So, how did you get into cooking?' Eros had enquired, strolling informally into the kitchen on her first night while she'd been preparing his evening meal, his every fluid movement attracting her attention, particularly to the fabric defining his long, powerful thighs.

'My mother was a cook and she started teaching me when I was five,' Winnie had confided as she'd struggled not to look back in the same direction, perplexed by her random thoughts and embarrassing impulses in his presence. 'Both my parents were Greek, although my mother's family had been living here for years when she met my father—'

'Yet you don't speak our language,' Eros had remarked in surprise.

Winnie had tensed, her eyes shadowing. 'My parents died when I was eight and I've forgotten most of the Greek words I knew. I've always meant to go to classes but I'm too busy. Some day I'll take it up again.'

'So, what are you making me tonight?' Eros had asked with a lazy smile, his accented drawl smooth as silk in her ears.

'I put a little menu on the dining table for you.'

'Cute,' Eros had commented with lancing amusement.

'Just tell me what you want and I'll provide it,' she had urged, eager to please for he had been paying generously for her services and she'd wanted him to feel that she was worth her salary.

An ebony brow had skated up. *'Anything?'* he had pressed, laughter sparkling in his spectacular eyes, his wide sensual mouth lifting at the corners.

'Pretty much anything,' Winnie had muttered, belatedly grasping the double entendre she had accidentally made, her colour rising accordingly. 'And if I don't know how to make it, I can soon find out.'

'Is your accommodation adequate?' Eros had prompted.

'It's lovely. Your housekeeper was very helpful,' Winnie had told him cheerfully, even though it had been something of a shock to enter a household where virtually no one had spoken any English and where she'd known she would be a little lonely. There had been few staff because Eros had been the only resident and had frequently been away from home. Only the housekeeper, Karena, had lived in and she had been near retirement age, besides having only a very basic grasp of English.

Karena's entry into the kitchen that evening had concluded that conversation with Eros, for the housekeeper had usually served the meals, but a couple of nights later when Winnie had noticed how very tired the older woman had looked, she had urged her to return to her flat for the night and leave her to serve the meal. It had been a strategic error to expose herself to greater contact with Eros but at the time she had felt guilty about the fat salary she earned and the reality that she worked much shorter hours than Karena, who had been on duty from dawn to dusk and busy even when Eros had been abroad because she'd overseen the cleaning and maintenance of the house. When Karena had fallen victim to a sprained wrist, that serving arrangement had become permanent with Karena departing to her flat every evening before Eros's return.

Only a few evenings had passed before Eros had suggested she join him and, although she had demurred in surprise and discomfiture the first time, the second time he had asked she had told herself that it would be rude to refuse again and she had sat down and shared a glass of wine with him. She had asked him about his day and his foreign travels and had listened while he'd talked, sipping her wine, answering the occasional query while becoming maddeningly aware of the intensity of his beautiful eyes on her. Just sitting there she had felt all hot and tingly, flattered by his interest, his apparent desire for her company when he could've had so many more glamorous women eagerly filling the same role.

Back then Winnie had been a retiring mixture of naivety and insecurity when men were around. Keen to climb the career ladder, she hadn't dated much, and as soon as her sisters had begun looking to her as a role model, dating had become even more of a challenge. A couple of unsavoury experiences with men who had wanted much more than she'd wanted to give had kept her a virgin. Working long, unsocial hours hadn't helped, so the thrill of being in Eros's company and the sole focus of his attention had rather gone to her head. The first kiss... *No*, she didn't want to remember that which loomed large in her memory as her first major mistake. Squashing that untimely recollection, she walked past the opulent vehicle that she assumed was Eros's limousine and was unlocking the front door of the house when she heard him behind her.

'An elegant location,' he remarked, making her jump as she hurriedly crossed the threshold.

'Yes, thanks to Grandad. The house belongs to him.' Hurriedly doffing her coat, Winnie hung it up in the alcove and showed him into the lounge. 'You can wait in here while I feed Teddy and put him down for his nap...'

'Why did you choose to call him Teddy?' he queried.

'Officially it's Theodore, my father's middle name,' she proffered stiffly. 'But it was too big a name for a baby and he ended up Teddy instead.'

Uninvited, Eros followed her into the kitchen, where she strapped Teddy into his booster seat at the table and whipped between fridge and microwave, warming her son's lunch while studiously ignoring Eros's silent presence by the door.

Teddy grasped his spoon and ate, making more of a mess than usual, showing off because a stranger was present.

'I assume your sisters look after him while you're at work?' Eros prompted.

'Yes…' Winnie glanced worriedly at him. 'They're very good with him.'

'A father would have been even better.'

Breathing in deep and slow to restrain her temper, Winnie concentrated on cleaning up Teddy and the table, unstrapping him to lift him.

'Allow me…' Disconcertingly, Eros stepped right into her path and simply scooped her son out of her hold. 'Where to now?'

'Upstairs,' Winnie said thinly, reluctantly leading the way.

She pushed open the door of Teddy's room.

'This is a little girl's room,' Eros objected, only slowly lowering her son into his cot, his attention pinned to the pink cartoon mural of princesses on the wall.

'We haven't got around to redecorating yet,' Winnie retorted, sidestepping the truth that the sisters had decided not to go to that trouble and expense when they were unsure how long their grandfather would allow them to make the house their home. Stepping over to the cot, she slipped off her son's shoes and his sweatshirt and settled him down before tugging the string on the little musical mobile that had been his from birth.

Closing the curtains, she walked back to the door, watching Eros hover by the cot. 'Why's the cot in the middle of the room?' he asked.

'Because if you put it beside the furniture, Teddy will use it to climb out and I don't want the hassle of trying to persuade him to stay put in a junior bed. He's too young to understand.'

'A nanny would remove much of the burden of childcare,' Eros commented smoothly. 'It must be hard for you to work and care adequately for him at the same time.'

'Not with my sisters around,' Winnie countered steadily, refusing to rise to the suggestion that she wasn't doing the best mothering job possible.

Eros strode down the stairs only a step in her wake and she walked into the lounge. 'I suppose I should offer you coffee,' she said stiffly.

Eros sent her a winging hard glance. 'No, thanks. Let's not procrastinate.'

'If you must know, I was trying to be polite.'

Eros shrugged a broad shoulder, the edge of his jacket falling back to expose a shirt front pulling taut across his muscular torso, delineating sleek bands of abdominal muscle. As she watched, her mouth ran dry and she looked hastily away, colour warming her cheeks.

'Why bother?' Eros incised drily. 'We're neither friends nor casual acquaintances.'

'What do you want from me?' Winnie fired back at him, anxiety biting through her.

'Answers,' Eros framed silkily. 'And I'll keep on coming back at you until I get them.'

CHAPTER THREE

'ANSWERS? WELL, I can give you a question. Why didn't you tell me that you were a married man?' Winnie demanded abruptly, infuriated by his refusal to acknowledge that deception.

'You never asked if I was married,' Eros pointed out smoothly.

And that fast, Winnie wanted to hit him, hit him so hard she knocked him into the middle of next week. Her small hands curled into tight fists, her cheeks pink with the force of her resentment and the galling knowledge that she couldn't afford to lose control of her temper. 'Why would I have asked when ostensibly you were living alone and there was no visible woman in your life?' she shot back at him. 'I hadn't the smallest suspicion that you were already in a relationship!'

'My marriage is not a subject I'm prepared to discuss with you,' Eros informed her arrogantly, clenching his strong jawline. 'I would have been willing to discuss that topic two years ago. But two years on, I don't believe I owe you that explanation.'

Winnie clenched her teeth together as hard as if she were biting into solid metal. 'Oh, don't you, indeed?' she exclaimed, vexed by that provocative assurance and, if anything, madder than ever.

'You met Tasha,' Eros acknowledged curtly. 'Eventually I did find that out and presumably that is why you chose to suddenly disappear without giving *me* any explanation.'

'Don't say that like it excuses you… *Nothing* excuses your behaviour!' Winnie slammed back at him furiously. 'And I didn't owe you anything!'

Eros studied her with intent, glittering green eyes. She still had lousy dress sense, he conceded ruefully, invariably choosing to envelop herself in drab colours and very practical clothing, but he knew her ripe body as well as he knew his own and he could see the changes in her lush figure, which even clad in leggings and an all-concealing sweatshirt was visibly fuller at breast and hip. He hardened, momentarily snatched back into hot, sweaty memories of the passion that had once threatened to consume him. His treacherous libido heated up, sending a sensual pulse through his groin and making him bite back a curse at his lack of restraint.

For a while, the sheer novelty of that passion had obsessed him and, having recognised that as a dan-

gerous weakness, he had refused to allow himself
to look for her after she vanished out of his life.
He could get by fine without sex; he had got by for
years and he no longer fell as easily into temptation as he had fallen with her. He was free now, he
reminded himself, but that old belief that he had
to always stay in control of his physical urges was
still ingrained in him. Giving way to those same
urges had destroyed his father's life. Winnie had
made him feel dangerously out of control and that,
if he was honest with himself, had unnerved him.

'At the very least, you owed me the knowledge
that you were pregnant with my child,' Eros delivered in harsh condemnation.

'No, I didn't!' Winnie slammed back at him in
annoyance. 'Your deception released me from any
such obligation!'

His stunning eyes narrowed, black velvety lashes
shading that mesmeric green. 'There was no deception on my part. For a deception to be contrived,
one must deliberately engage in concealment of the
truth…and I did not. I didn't tell you a single lie!'

For several unbearable seconds, Winnie searched
her memory for evidence of a lie and her inability
to find one merely enraged her more. He was so
scheming, so specious in his arguments. 'But you
also knew I hadn't the faintest suspicion that you
were a married man!' she flung back at him bitterly.

Eros inclined his glossy dark head. 'Did I?

Some women are content to sleep with married men without questioning their status.'

'Stop playing with words!' Winnie interrupted, rising up on her toes, pulsing with angry tension. 'That's what you're doing in defiance of the facts! You knew I wasn't *that* kind of woman… You knew I wouldn't willingly get involved with a married man!'

Again, Eros shrugged, the lean, hard angles of his sculpted features set like granite. 'None of this nonsense is pertinent now,' he claimed in a dry tone of finality. 'I will not engage in a slanging match about our past. That ship sailed a long time ago. What is germane now is that you have my son and you didn't tell me about him. Let's concentrate on that, rather than on facts we cannot change.'

Winnie tore her gaze from him with difficulty and turned her head away, momentarily at a loss. In one sense he was correct, in that there was nothing to be gained from arguing about what had happened between them two years earlier, but that also meant that he was denying her any justification for having chosen not to inform him of her pregnancy. Her slight shoulders stiffened and her head swung back, dark strands of her lush mane of hair falling across cheeks flushed by angry frustration.

'How did you become pregnant anyway?' Eros

demanded without warning. 'I *always* took precautions.'

At that much-too-intimate question, Winnie practically fried in mortification inside her own burning skin and she walked stiffly over to the window, momentarily turning her back on him. 'No, there were times when you overlooked that necessity,' she told him grudgingly, forced to recall early-morning encounters when she had wakened to his hard, thrillingly aroused body pressed to hers and in warm drowsy lust and need had succumbed without either of them thinking of contraception.

'I don't remember a single occasion,' Eros informed her with a raw edge to his dark, deep, accented drawl.

'Then you must have a very short memory because I remember at least a dozen occasions when contraception was the last thing on your mind. In the shower, in the pool, early mornings when we were both half-asleep.' Winnie forced out the words like staccato bullets voiced between gritted teeth. 'In fact, you were downright careless, and I noticed but I didn't say anything. Instead, I tried to go on the pill to protect myself but by the time I saw a GP, it was too late. I had already conceived.'

'You should've drawn those oversights to my attention,' Eros delivered curtly, reflecting that if anything should've warned him that the affair was

out of control, it was exactly that aberrant careless-
ness on his part that underlined it. He had got too
comfortable with her, too *involved* to be logical
and safe. It had been a high-voltage sexual affair
and he hadn't been prepared for it, hadn't counted
the risks or the costs, had simply waded in like a
man with an unquenchable thirst and drunk so
deep that even his intelligence was compromised.

Winnie twisted back to him in a sudden movement. 'Oh, really?' she carolled tartly. 'So, the fact
I fell pregnant is my fault too, is it?'

'There's little point in awarding blame this late
in the day,' Eros murmured curtly. 'What is done
is done and we have a child…a child who is, sadly,
a stranger to me. That must be remedied immediately.'

Winnie was so rigid that her very muscles ached
with the strain. 'Must it?'

'Of course, it must be,' Eros declared, studying her with an incredulity that implied she would
have to be witless to expect anything else. 'Teddy
must learn that I am his father and I need to get
to know him. I would like to spend time with him
tomorrow.'

'No,' Winnie cut in without even thinking about
it because Teddy had always been hers and he had
never been in the care of anyone outside the family.

'Naturally, I will bring a qualified nanny with
me to ensure that Teddy's basic needs are properly

met while he is with me. I have a lot to learn about being a father,' Eros admitted with a candour that disconcerted her. 'But given time and experience, I will pick up what I have to know.'

'I really can't believe that you're *this* interested in Teddy!' Winnie proclaimed in consternation, watching him pace back and forth in front of her, the lithe grace of his every movement strikingly noticeable and grabbing her attention with its aching familiarity.

A hollow sensation opened inside Winnie, her breath suddenly tripping in her throat. Her nipples were peaking, suddenly tender and tight beneath her clothing. She dragged in a jagged breath as the hot melting sensation of arousal pulsed between her taut thighs. How did he do that to her? How on earth could he still do that to her when she knew he was no longer hers to crave? Never had been hers either, except in her imagination, she reminded herself guiltily, dragging her attention from him to try to focus elsewhere.

'Obviously I want to get to know my son and I expect that process to begin immediately,' Eros spelt out bluntly. 'I will not accept you putting obstacles in my path.'

'Is that a fact?' Winnie sizzled back at him, feeling as though she was under attack on every front.

'I am being frank. You have denied me my rights as a parent for quite long enough,' Eros reasoned. 'The situation must change. I will see Teddy tomorrow and take him out. He will be very well taken care of.'

'I'll come too,' Winnie broke in insistently. 'You won't need a nanny.'

'No,' Eros countered decisively, his wide sensual lips compressing into a determined line. 'I would prefer to get to know my son away from your influence.'

'He's too young for that yet!' Winnie argued passionately. 'He's never been away from me before.'

'Then it is time you encouraged him to achieve a little independence.'

'He's only a baby!' Winnie gasped defensively.

'He will come to no harm in my care. He is my son, my family, indeed the only close family I have left alive,' Eros pointed out grittily. 'Obviously he will be looked after to the very best of my ability.'

'You *can't* simply exclude me!' Winnie said accusingly.

Eros elevated a winged ebony brow in direct challenge. 'Is that not what you have done to me?' he pressed silkily. 'I have been excluded from every aspect of his life since birth but that cannot continue and you have to accept that reality.'

'I don't have to accept anything from you!' Winnie objected vehemently, wondering how they had contrived to travel so swiftly from rehashing old issues to his shattering demand to have full unsupervised access to their son.

And that was the crux of the matter, Winnie registered belatedly. Teddy was *their* son, not only hers, not only his. It was truly the first time that she had been confronted by the unwelcome truth that she did not have total, unbreakable rights over her own child and that awareness cut through her like a knife blade, giving rise to all sorts of other worries and insecurities. Faster than the speed of light, Eros was interfering, setting down his boundaries and making unapologetic demands. Eros was not the sort of man likely to humbly sit back in the corner and wait until she decided to cede him his rights as a parent.

'You have to learn to share Teddy,' Eros intoned without hesitation. 'But try starting your judgement of me from a *fair* starting point. Why assume that I won't look after my son as well as you do?'

'I didn't make that assumption,' Winnie contradicted nervously. 'I'm just warning you now that, no matter how well you look after him, Teddy will fret away from me and that you'll find him a handful.'

'You would like me to have difficulties handling him,' Eros assumed grimly, shooting her an unimpressed glance. 'But I do not foresee a problem.'

'Have you any experience in looking after a child this young?' Winnie enquired, needled by his insuperable confidence.

'No. You must know that I am an only child and few of my friends are parents yet,' Eros admitted grudgingly. 'But with a trained childcare professional on hand to advise me, I am sure that we will manage.'

'Teddy's at an unpredictable age. He throws tantrums,' Winnie warned him ruefully. 'He can go from rage to tears in seconds.'

'Perhaps my son needs more stable and reliable care to thrive,' Eros murmured silkily, as if tantrums could only be the consequence of inadequate parenting.

In receipt of that covert criticism, Winnie reddened with furious resentment. 'As you said yourself, you have a lot to learn about children,' she responded non-committally, however, reluctant to expose her sensitivity to any questioning of her own parenting skills. She wondered if she was a complete shrew to hope that Teddy would lose his rag with Eros and teach him the reality of dealing with a volatile toddler.

'And tomorrow evening, after I have returned Teddy to your care, we will have dinner together and discuss—like reasonable adults—where to go from here,' Eros decreed decisively.

Winnie compressed her lips. If Eros wanted access to Teddy, she supposed that they had to discuss arrangements that would be acceptable to both of them. But how would she cope with that when even the prospect of having to part with Teddy for a few hours the next day daunted her? She knew that she would spend the entire time Teddy was away from her worrying about him.

'We'll have to dine out some other time,' she told him and not without a certain satisfaction. 'I have to work tomorrow evening.'

'I'm leaving for New York the next day and I will be away for at least a week. A later date will not be convenient for me,' Eros told her levelly. 'Get a night off or plead sickness. It's up to you.'

'I won't do that, Eros. I won't let my employers down.'

'Do you know where I'm going from here?' Eros enquired grimly. 'To consult my lawyer about my legal position with regard to Teddy. You are not in a strong enough position to be difficult, Winnie. We *must* discuss provisions and soon.'

Her heart-shaped face pulled taut, her big brown eyes suddenly ducking from his as she strove to withstand the conviction that she was being deliberately intimidated and forced in a direction in which she had no desire to go. 'Are you threatening me?' she asked curtly, feeling a little like a wayward farm animal being firmly herded down a preset track.

'No. I'm being *honest*,' Eros fielded with harsh emphasis. 'I am impatient to get to know my son and I would advise you not to stand in the way of that desire. It is natural for a new father to be keen to establish a normal relationship with his child.'

'But this keen interest of yours is coming at me out of nowhere!' Winnie protested hotly.

'Your vengeful attitude ends here and now,' Eros breathed in a raw undertone.

Winnie flung her head back to look up at him, having until that moment somehow contrived to forget how very tall he was in comparison to her. He was also way too close for comfort, the faint, dangerously familiar scent of his designer cologne flaring her nostrils. 'What on earth are you talking about?' she demanded blankly. *'Vengeful?'* she questioned with incredulous emphasis on that choice of word.

'When you found out that I was married, you decided to punish me by withholding all knowledge of my child from me,' Eros extended with perceptible bitterness, his lean, darkly handsome face sardonic.

'That's nonsense!' Winnie proclaimed in shocked denial. 'I'm not that sort of person!'

'You believed that the fact I was a married man was a good enough excuse to exclude me from Teddy's life. But it wasn't. That attitude won't wash with me now. You have to adapt to a new situation.'

'And what about your situation? How is your wife going to feel about all this?' Winnie cut across his condemnatory speech to demand helplessly. 'How is *she* going to react to Teddy's existence?'

'I don't have a wife any longer. I've been divorced for some time,' Eros informed her grimly. 'All matters concerning Teddy are between you and I and nobody else.'

Winnie was shocked, having automatically assumed he was still married. From the minute she had discovered that Eros was married, she had suppressed every inappropriate urge to look him up on the Internet and learn, not only about his marriage, but about what he was doing. He belonged to another woman. He was no longer her business, should *never* have been her business. She had warned herself painfully, fearing that seeking information about him would only fuel her longing for him.

She had been too ashamed of her behaviour at having slept with another woman's husband to allow herself to give way to further temptation. Her sin had been unintentional and born out of ignorance, but the guilt of that mistake still sat very heavily on her conscience. Indeed, that wanton fling with Eros had taught her to police her every thought. She had learned not to rush into judgement of others for their mistakes. She had learned that she could be as weak and imperfect as the most foolish of women when she fell in love, all tough lessons she could've done without.

She didn't properly breathe again until Eros had left, leaving her at the mercy of insecurity and stress. Eros had always had the ability to take her by surprise and slash through her calm controlled front with ease, unearthing the much more vulnerable woman she was underneath. That acknowledgement plunged her into the steamy memory of their first kiss.

Eros had been abroad for a couple of weeks and he had walked into the kitchen to greet her, insisting that she join him for a glass of wine again, a familiarity that her sane mind had already been questioning. There was such a thing as getting *too* friendly and informal with an employer, she had reasoned unhappily, and she had been on the brink of pulling back and making polite excuses. And then Eros had stalked into the kitchen, clearly looking for her, all bristling energy and impatience, and he had smiled at her, that breathtakingly warm smile that literally made her heart beat so fast she felt breathless.

Without further ado, he had snatched her up off her sensible feet as if she were a doll while she was still muttering naively about the special dessert she had prepared. His mouth had plunged down on hers, full of a hot demanding hunger that had set her treacherous body alight. She'd had butterflies in her tummy and had been in a daze with her entire being vibrating from that explosively sensual assault as he had slowly lowered her to the tiles again, her body brushing down against every lean, powerful inch of his. She had been viscerally aware of the hard thrust of desire that not even the most exquisitely tailored suit could conceal.

'I want you so much,' Eros had said simply. 'I missed you. I've never missed a woman like this before.'

And it had been the very simplicity of that admission that had seduced her because she had missed him too, missed those quiet, private little moments of peace and tranquillity in his company. Instead of stepping back, instead of exercising good judgement, she had joined him for the wine, even shared that wretched dessert with him, laughing when he'd teased her about her professional pride in her creations. She could've told him then that nothing had inspired her with greater pride than his evident interest in her ordinary self. When it was late, when it was past time for her to be retiring for the evening she had reluctantly stood up, and he had stood up as well and reached for her.

'Stay with me tonight,' he had urged, and he had kissed her again.

It was the first time she had gone upstairs in that house and she had gone into his palatial bedroom with him, trembling with nerves, questioning her decision every step of the way even while her body had burned with eagerness and wanton impatience to finally know what other women knew. The die had been cast at that moment. She had been a push-over, falling in love and already trustingly invest-ing Eros with far more importance in her life than he'd been investing in her.

Looking back, she believed that Eros had merely been taking advantage of an available woman. It was even possible that the prospect of taking her virginity had turned him on because he had known she was inexperienced, had guessed, reassuring her even as she had anxiously admitted it. Noth-ing could have prepared her for the passionate ex-citement that had followed or the deep sense of closeness she'd felt afterwards with him. From that night on, she had been at the mercy of her emo-tions and common sense hadn't got a look-in.

Her sisters returned from work, eager to hear what had happened between her and Eros. Zoe took an optimistic view, deeming it healthy that Teddy's father and her sister were talking and a positive sign that Eros should be so interested in immedi-ately connecting with his son.

'But what is his end game?' Vivi probed with innate suspicion.

'Presumably what he says…getting to know Teddy, spending time with him,' Winnie pointed out awkwardly as she darted about her bedroom, getting ready for work. 'What else can he get out of this?'

'He strikes me as the sort of guy who always puts himself first,' Vivi declared with a curled lip. 'What's in it for him? There must be more than what we know. All of this is very coincidental. Does he know that Stam Fotakis is our grandfather?'

'No, it was never discussed. I'll mention it tomorrow, see how he reacts,' Winnie said ruefully. 'How am I going to hand Teddy over to him and some strange nanny tomorrow?'

'With kid gloves and a brave smile,' Zoe told her wryly. 'Let's hope the nanny is experienced.'

'Mama… Mama!' Teddy wailed pathetically.

That and the shouted 'Not baby!' when they tried to persuade him into his buggy were virtually the only words Eros had heard from his son. Oh, and there was the word *no*, which Teddy was even more partial to employing. He had neither volume control nor a need for privacy when he aired his innermost feelings. Teddy didn't care how many people were around when he flung himself down on the path and screamed blue murder for his mother. And he didn't like the nanny, physically fighting her if she tried to lift him, refusing to be distracted when she tried to tempt him out of the scenes he made.

But the advantage of Teddy distrusting the unfortunate nanny was that he clung to his slightly more familiar father as if his life depended on it. More positively, Teddy had loved the monkey enclosure at the zoo, he loved chocolate and he loved playgrounds. He was a smart little boy, energetic but explosive too. He was also so attached to his mother that he was forcing his father to rethink his tentative plans to challenge, should it prove possible, his mother's full-time custody.

But now Eros could see that there was no way Teddy would be happy, even on a part-time basis, to be deprived of Winnie. Shared custody definitely wasn't the path to take. Teddy needed Winnie as he needed air to breathe. Winnie was patently the very centre of Teddy's little world and the bedrock of his security and Eros knew that he would never do anything to hurt or harm his son. When he had even briefly considered his chances of parting mother from child, had he too been guilty of vengeful thinking? Eros asked himself grimly as they headed back early from their day out to reunite Teddy with Winnie. Eros knew that he now had to change his attitude and, for the sake of his son, consider a solution he had never dreamt he would be required to contemplate.

Marriage. Bearing in mind his past experience, just the thought of marriage brought Eros out in a cold sweat. He didn't want to get married again. In fact, he had promised himself that he would *never* marry again, reasoning that that was a rational decision when he had neither a family to please nor any desire to reproduce. He hadn't cared what happened to his business empire after he was gone, had never been vain enough to hope that he might merit a footnote in history. And then he had found out about Teddy and the whole picture of his life, his expectations and goals, had changed radically overnight.

'You'll be with Mama soon,' Eros soothed Teddy as his son let loose a choked sob that warned another distressed outburst was threatening.

'He's very attached to her,' the nanny commented.

'Too young to be separated from her,' Eros agreed, wishing he had listened to Winnie instead of arrogantly assuming that she would selfishly do everything she could to come between him and his son.

'With practice at socialising he would improve. A play group and the company of other children would be good for him,' the nanny opined.

'We'll see.'

Eros was forcing himself to think over Stam Fotakis's outrageous proposition from a different angle. He could live without owning the island of Trilis, however he could not live without his son being a regular part of his life. At the same time, if he was to be forced to marry Winnie anyway to gain consistent access to Teddy, why shouldn't he reclaim Trilis as part of the deal?

Even so, he refused to marry Winnie on the kind of terms that her grandfather had suggested, as a mere prelude to *another* divorce. If he married her, it would have to be a *real* marriage and both his wife and his child would naturally live with him. How would Winnie feel about that option?

Did that matter? Did he even care? Eros liked to win and he had no intention of meekly meeting the old man's unreasonable demands and surrendering his son. By all accounts, Stam Fotakis had been a pretty poor father to his own two sons and Eros did not want him taking charge of Teddy. If there was something in the marriage for Eros, however, sufficient to compensate him for the loss of his freedom, now that was a different matter, he mused thoughtfully. Teddy *and* Winnie, not to mention the family island in the package, now that was a deal worthy of consideration by any hot-blooded man. He wondered, though, just how much pressure he would have to put on Winnie to achieve that package and then shelved the thought, broodingly reminding himself that she deserved whatever she got for denying him his son…

CHAPTER FOUR

'How do I look?' Winnie asked her siblings.

'Scared,' Vivi declared bluntly.

Winnie smoothed damp palms down over her ample hips and looked nervously in the mirror. The dress was wine red, purchased for their trip to Greece to meet their grandfather, the stretchy fabric hugging her curves to define every ounce of excess weight. And there *was* excess, she thought ruefully, because she had yet to lose all the extra pounds she had gained during pregnancy. Her long hours, the high-powered pressure of working in a busy kitchen and the irregular, often snatched meals had all played havoc with her intention to get back down to her original weight. 'I look fat,' she said curtly.

'It's not a date,' Vivi pointed out drily.

'You are *not* fat,' Zoe protested. 'You're just small and curvy and obviously he likes that.'

'Doesn't matter what *he* likes!' Vivi interrupted.

'If he tries to lay a finger on you, scream the place down, Winnie!'

'Vivi,' Winnie said gently, her sister's drama ironically calming her. 'Eros and I can barely speak to each other politely. He's hardly likely to make a pass at me. That's not what this is about.'

'Well, be careful about what you agree to,' the redhead warned her. 'We don't want to lose Teddy every weekend just because you're usually working.'

'I won't agree to anything tonight. I'll ask for time to think over any suggestion he makes.'

'Don't be late. You have to get up early tomorrow,' Zoe reminded her.

The sisters were catching the train down to John and Liz's home for their regular monthly catch-up with their former foster parents. Their grandfather had bought out the couple's mortgage to ensure that the house wasn't repossessed but he had refused to sign the property over to John and Liz until his granddaughters had met his terms and married. Winnie suppressed a troubled sigh as she slid her feet into vertiginous sparkly heels borrowed from Zoe and never worn. Zoe loved glitter and sparkle but had to be dragged at gunpoint into social situations.

Winnie thought ruefully about the financial difficulties that had plunged the Brookes into crisis. After John had suffered a stroke, money had been in short supply for years afterwards. John's plumbing business had failed, leaving the kindly couple deep in debt. Although he had eventually made an excellent physical recovery, they had been unable to meet their mortgage payments and they had fallen behind until eventually they had been facing the loss of their home.

Reminding herself soothingly that that worry was currently at bay, thanks to their grandfather, Winnie left the house and climbed into the taxi waiting outside for her. Eros had phoned her to tell her she would be picked up, his dark, deep voice cool and very much to the point. Why did that make her recall Eros practically purring down the phone as he'd chatted to her when he'd been far from home? In all, she had only known him for a few months. It had been a meaningless fling for him, she told herself impatiently, refusing to idealise what they had once shared. Their affair, as such, had stretched over two months and had encompassed long weekends spent together but Eros had often had to travel abroad.

The taxi dropped her off at a contemporary apartment block and she travelled up in the lift to the penthouse, her mouth dry as a bone as she contemplated seeing Eros again. He was Teddy's sperm donor, she instructed herself sourly, nothing more.

A manservant ushered her into a large open-plan

space tiled in limestone, sparsely furnished and showcasing several modern artworks. Her coat and scarf were taken while she curiously scanned her surroundings, surprised to find Eros occupying such a contemporary setting. His country house had been late Georgian and, like his spacious city town house, traditional in decor. Of course, he was divorced and single again, she reminded herself resolutely, and it was perfectly possible that the historic properties had been more his wife's style than his.

Yet where had his wife been all those many months while she was working for Eros? In Greece, only seeing him on special occasions? Winnie ground her teeth together, angrily stamping out her curiosity while scolding herself for her lack of discipline in allowing her mind to wander. She could not afford to be woolly-minded, or sentimentally slipping back into the past around a man as shrewd and quick to take advantage as Eros Nevrakis.

'Would you like a drink before dinner?' Eros enquired from behind her, forcing her to spin round in surprise, and in doing so she almost overbalanced in the very high heels she had worn in an effort to look taller…and therefore slimmer.

Eros reached out an arm as strong as steel and clamped it to her side to steady her, long fingers biting into the curve of her hip. Of course, he was noticing that there was more value to every pound of her than there had been two years earlier, she mocked herself, knocked off balance by his proximity. Bigger was bigger and couldn't be concealed.

'Thanks… Er… I don't mind if I do,' she muttered uneasily, stepping back from him in haste.

Eros, already entranced by her back view, was practically mesmerised by the front view. The thin fabric outlined her superb violin curves, enclosing lush full breasts, a still-tiny waist and a glorious rounded bottom. *Ne*… Yes, there was more of her but it was a voluptuously *sexy* more that sent lust rocketing through him.

Hugely self-conscious beneath that keen green-eyed appraisal, Winnie pushed her hair back from her brow.

'You've grown your hair,' Eros remarked.

'Too busy to go to the hairdresser,' she parried awkwardly, studying him nervously from below her lashes, afraid to be caught in the act of staring.

For, my goodness, Eros deserved to be stared at. Clad in designer jeans that cupped his lean hips and faithfully outlined every sleek line of his long muscular legs, and a silver-grey shirt that defined the width of his shoulders and the breadth of his powerful torso, he was dazzlingly male. Winnie clutched the glass of wine he gave her, grateful to have something to occupy her hands.

'Teddy's a terrific little boy,' he commented, surprising her with that compliment.

Winnie nodded, managing a smile. 'I think so too,' she said inanely and then winced for herself.

'Obviously we both want what's best for him and we want to make him happy,' Eros intoned.

'The road to hell is paved with good intentions,' Winnie muttered ruefully. 'Please don't overwhelm Teddy. Let him get to know you in his own good time. He's like most young kids—he doesn't adapt well to sudden changes in his routine.'

'That's a tall order. I spend most of my time in Greece,' Eros volunteered, glancing at the manservant now lodged in the doorway. 'I believe our meal is ready.'

'You used to spend most of your time in London,' Winnie remarked, settling down at the polished, beautifully set table to look at her exquisitely presented starter without appetite. But then nerves always squashed her hunger, she reflected, even if nerves had never squashed her hunger for him.

It was not an acknowledgement she was keen to make but there it was, the elephant in the room that couldn't be ignored. Colliding with those black-fringed green eyes of his, she experienced what could only be likened to a sugar rush of excitement. It made her feel like a feckless teenager and a flush of chagrin coloured her face as she firmly focused her attention on her food.

'My base is in Greece now,' Eros informed her

smoothly. 'I wouldn't be able to spend much time with my son here.'

Winnie stiffened, since there was nothing she could do about that problem. 'That's unfortunate,' she said awkwardly.

'But not an insuperable problem,' Eros murmured silkily.

'Good,' she said hastily, tension lancing through her more sharply than ever as if there was some invisible threat nearby that she had to watch out for.

The threat was Eros, of course it was, all male, all powerful, arrogant Eros, who liked to order his world exactly as he liked it and who would very much dislike anything or anyone who got in his way. 'Who's cooking for you now?' she asked brightly, keen to dial down the intensity of the dialogue with a man who could somehow make the simplest statements sound ominous, making gooseflesh prickle at the back of her neck.

'I had food sent in tonight from one of my favourite restaurants. I'm not here often enough now to maintain a permanent chef,' he admitted as the second course arrived and the manservant topped up their wine glasses.

And there it was, she thought melodramatically, Eros exerting control again. He had smoothly brought the thorny topic of his rare visits to London right back to where they had started and placed it before her again like a reproach, cutting through her attempt to sidetrack him.

'You may know my paternal grandfather,' Winnie remarked abruptly, determined not to fall into the trap of shouldering blame for *his* unavailability to act as a regular father. 'Stamboulas Fotakis. My sisters and I only met him recently.'

Eros's scrutiny was level and cool and uniquely uninformative. 'Who hasn't heard of Bull Fotakis? He's a legend in his own lifetime. Why didn't you mention that connection two years ago?'

Winnie laid down her knife and fork and grasped her glass. 'To be honest, mentioning it never even crossed my mind. At that point I hadn't met him or, indeed, had any contact with him. My father parted with him on bad terms but we don't have any other relatives. My sisters were too young when my parents died to appreciate that we did have a grandparent still living. When I told them about him, they were curious and keen to get to know him,' she said truthfully. 'We are very grateful for the house he allows us to live in.'

The lean, strong lineaments of his darkly handsome face had pulled taut. 'It's my job to be keeping you and my child, *not* your grandfather's,' he declared bluntly.

He would make a terrific poker player, she thought wryly, for he had betrayed no strong reaction to her admission of her grandfather's identity, indeed had merely turned the spotlight straight back to himself.

'That's a rather old-fashioned outlook, if you don't mind me saying,' Winnie dared, pausing to sip her wine and refresh her dry mouth.

'I *do* mind you saying it,' Eros countered, green eyes glittering like shards of sea glass between lush black lashes. 'My son and the mother of my child are solely my responsibility. There's nothing old-fashioned about that conviction. Even the law would back me up. *I* should be maintaining both of you.'

Winnie paled, her appetite dwindling even more beneath the sheer weight of his gaze. He was *so* intense and Teddy emanated that same intensity in whatever he did, suggesting that it was a family trait. 'Let's not argue,' she muttered uneasily, gathering that he was planning to persuade her to accept financial help from him.

'Undoubtedly, we will find much to argue about,' Eros told her, dismaying her with his insouciance at that prospect because Winnie was no fan of conflict, particularly around Teddy. 'Eat up,' he urged lightly.

'Why is it so important for you to be a big part of Teddy's life?' Winnie pressed more boldly.

'My father divorced my mother when I was eight and I barely saw him after that,' Eros admitted, disconcerting her with that admission. 'He remarried and my stepmother had no interest in kids. That marriage broke down, as well. My father lived a chaotic life after he left my mother and he didn't have the time or the energy to continue being a parent. By the time I was eighteen and he was dying, he was a stranger.'

Winnie winced. 'I'm sorry. I had no idea.'

'But perhaps you will now understand why I see my role in Teddy's life as being a role of crucial importance for his benefit as well as mine,' he murmured sibilantly, his eyes veiled, his expression grave.

'Yes,' she conceded reluctantly. 'Yes, I can see that an absent father would leave an impression on you.'

'Fortunately for me, when I was setting up my first business, I met an older man who acted as my mentor and steered me away from more imprudent investments,' he admitted wryly. 'Without Filipe's backing, my first venture would have run aground. He was the father my own father was too busy and selfish to be. I don't ever want my son to view me in that light.'

'Naturally not,' Winnie agreed, pushing her plate away.

Involuntarily, she was entranced by the informative glimpse he was giving her of his younger years because Eros had always been very tight-lipped about his background. He had backed away or ignored intrusive questions and if she persisted, he had shut her down with brooding silence. He had stubbornly resisted her once-overwhelming desire to know everything there was to know about him, but then possibly he had been afraid that he might stumble if he talked too freely and accidentally reveal that he was married. Nothing would ever persuade her that he had kept that dark secret unintentionally.

She watched him eat his dessert with eyes that brimmed with growing amusement and memories. Eros had a very sweet tooth. He only ever indulged it at mealtimes and she knew he worked hard in the gym to stay lean and fit. He ushered her back into the comfortable living area, carrying her wine for her.

Winnie grew apprehensive again, sensing that Eros was about to state his demands with regard to their son. He strolled over to the windows and opened the doors onto the balcony, allowing the sounds of the world outside to intrude. She followed him out onto the roof garden, clutching her glass like a lifeline and settling down in a padded seat while he leant up against the balustrade, unperturbed by the light breeze tousling his black curls.

'I've reached the conclusion that we should get married,' Eros murmured silkily and without the smallest effort to prepare her for that startling announcement. 'It would settle every problem and then we could both support Teddy.'

Winnie froze in shock and stared at him, huge brown eyes welded to his lean dark features and the brilliance of his intense green eyes. Memories unravelled inside her head, tossing her back in time, momentarily burying her in intimate recollections. Eros always looked most alert in the grip of passion and she sensed that for some reason the idea of marrying her fell into that same category of being something he wanted a great deal. Why, she had no idea, but she was convinced that it was truly important to him. Certainly not for sex or for her own self, she gathered, since he had let her walk out of his life two years earlier and made no attempt to see her again. Finding her when she had only moved back in with her sisters wouldn't have been that much of a challenge for Eros. But at best on his terms, she had only been a fling and at worst, a casual mistress, not a woman he either needed or really cared about and he hadn't looked for her.

'Why do you think that we should marry?' she almost croaked, her throat dry with stress and confusion.

'Teddy.' Eros shrugged a shoulder. 'There's no other way to give him everything he needs.'

'That's nonsensical!' Winnie objected boldly. 'Loads of couples live separate lives and share their children perfectly happily.'

'And how are we going to share Teddy when I'm based in Greece?' Eros derided.

'That's not my problem,' Winnie told him thinly. 'Maybe you could start spending more time here?'

'I asked you to marry me,' Eros reminded her very drily. 'Don't you think you should be a little more gracious?'

An angry flush of chagrin mantled Winnie's cheekbones. Suspicion infiltrated her, swiftly followed by comprehension. Hadn't she just told him that one of the richest men in the world was her grandfather? In Eros's eyes, she had evidently become an eligible bride because she was no longer a penniless cook. 'No, I don't,' she snapped back resentfully. 'You certainly wouldn't have asked me to marry you two years ago!'

'Not unless I wished to be tried as a bigamist,' he fielded with sardonic bite. 'I wasn't free to marry then and Teddy didn't exist. But now we have Teddy to consider and I would like my son to carry my name.'

'He's perfectly happy with *my* name!' Winnie parried with spirit. 'You know very well that you don't *really* want to marry me, Eros. I'm just a woman you slept with who became inconveniently pregnant.'

Eros ignored that statement. 'I want my son in my home and I can't have him *without* his mother.'

Winnie lost her angry colour and dropped her gaze, the pain of rejection slicing through her. 'Oh, thank you very much,' she framed curtly.

'*Thee mou…*' Eros growled in sudden seething frustration. 'Of course I want you too!'

Winnie rose from her seat and set her glass down with a sharp little snap. 'Well, maybe…just maybe, Mr Ego, I don't want you!' she slung back.

'It would take me only five minutes to prove otherwise,' Eros bit out in unhesitating challenge. 'Let me list all the many reasons why we should marry.'

'Oh, spare me the lecture, please,' Winnie muttered witheringly. 'Or why not start with the fact that the idea would never have occurred to you if I hadn't told you that I was related to Stam Fotakis?'

Eros stared back at her in shock, noticeably turning pale beneath his bronzed skin, the angles of his high cheekbones starkly prominent and taut. 'You actually think I want you for the money you may one day inherit?' he breathed in incredulous rage.

No, definitely not a gold-digger, Winnie decided, reckoning that no man could fake that amount of disbelief and outrage. It was time for her to bow smartly out of their civil little dinner date before they came to physical blows. 'I think I should go home now.'

A hand closed round hers and jerked her back around before she could walk indoors again. Shimmering sea-glass eyes locked to her flushed face like lasers. 'This has *nothing* to do with you being a member of the Fotakis family. This is between us.'

'Well, no, actually it's not,' Winnie argued, dry-mouthed with tension. 'This is about you wanting Teddy and having to take me too and apparently make the best of a bad bargain.'

'*Thee mou*... Where are your wits?' Eros growled down at her with lancing impatience. 'I want you.'

'You didn't want me so much that you came looking for me two years ago!' Winnie flared back at him in an outburst that, despite her best efforts, emerged as accusing in tone.

'I was married. Our relationship was wrong. That is why I didn't seek you out again,' Eros breathed in a fierce undertone. 'I didn't want to be tempted back into our affair.'

'A pity you didn't feel like that when you first met me!' Winnie tossed back at him accusingly. 'We'd all have been a lot happier if you'd done the right thing from the start!'

'But we wouldn't have had Teddy,' Eros pointed out unarguably. 'And now that I have met him, I wouldn't change the past even if I could.'

Alarmingly conscious of the hand closed round her narrow wrist, the fingers lazily stroking her arm as if to soothe her, Winnie dropped her head, knowing that in spite of the unhappiness Eros had caused her, she would never wish that Teddy had not been born because he had brought so much love, light and comfort into the world with him. Eros had broken her heart but Teddy had healed her, giving her the focus and the strength to rebuild her life.

'I *do* want you,' Eros grated, pushing up her chin, green eyes blazing bright as crystal in sunlight, crushing her soft full mouth under his, tasting her with a ravenous hunger that electrified her where she stood.

Her lips parted and something tightened deep down inside her pelvis as his tongue plunged into the sensitive interior of her mouth. A faint tremor racked her, her tongue tangling with his, her body instinctively straining towards him. Her breasts were full and tender and the burst of heat between her thighs compelled her headlong into his lean, muscular length, craving the contact that that overwhelming hunger had unleashed. The hard thrust of his arousal against her stomach was unmistakeable.

The sure, deft exploration of his hands over the swell of her bottom and then up over her tender breasts, cupping, squeezing, partially soothed the raw need traversing her and yet simultaneously drove it even higher. A whimper of choked sound was wrenched from her throat. She was utterly lost in the powerful sensations coursing through her, urging her on and destroying her every defence because what she was feeling was utterly mindless.

'Look at me…' Eros urged, his dark, deep, insistent drawl sending a tingling sensation down her taut spine. 'I want you. You want me. It's very simple.'

With a mighty mental exertion, Winnie forced her body back from the lure of his and stepped back a further pace for good measure. Her cheeks were burning with mortification and inside herself she was beating herself up for revelling in that kiss. 'No, it's not simple.'

'But it could be if we both act like reasonable people,' Eros intoned. 'I don't want to be forced into a custody battle with you.'

Winnie froze. 'C-custody?' she stammered in horror. 'Battle? Why would you do that?'

'Because if you say no to marriage, I have no other option,' Eros replied without hesitation. 'I want Teddy in my life, Winnie, and I won't settle for anything less.'

Winnie was pale and still in retreat from him. 'Obviously I'm willing to agree arrangements for you to see Teddy,' she reminded him. 'I wouldn't have come tonight if I hadn't been willing.'

His lean dark features were shuttered and hard. 'Occasional meetings here in London? That's not enough. I want more.'

Winnie steeled her backbone to stay upright and

she stared back at him, struggling to conceal her horror at the pressure he was putting on her. 'You can't have more,' she told him flatly. 'You can see Teddy whenever you're able but I won't agree to anything beyond that.'

His extraordinary eyes narrowed to glittering shards of green. 'Then we go to court and, be warned, I will arm myself with every piece of ammunition that I can lay my hands on to strengthen my own case...'

'You're threatening me,' she whispered shakily, a chill spreading through her body from deep down inside her, surprise and fear assailing her in a sickening wave.

'You're leaving my child in the care of a woman who was accused of working in a brothel, her name and her face plastered all over the gutter press!' Eros condemned.

Winnie, literally, felt faint with shock that he should already be aware of that embarrassing truth. He was talking about her sister Vivi, poor Vivi, whose first job had inadvertently led to her reputation being ruined. Vivi had believed she was working for a modelling agency but in fact it had also been an escort agency, which was raided by the police and closed down for operating illegally as a brothel. Being both photogenic and naive, Vivi had been branded as a prostitute by the tabloids as she was seen fleeing the premises that same day.

'And your other sister, who rarely goes out in public and suffers from panic attacks. How safe is Teddy with *her*?' Eros enquired lethally. 'What if she has one of those attacks when she's supposed to be looking after my son?'

'I hate you!' Winnie ground out rawly, anger splintering through her like a lightning bolt, for there was nothing she would not do to protect her younger sisters. 'How did you find out such confidential details about my family?'

'Such details are available to anyone with the cash to have you investigated,' Eros told her levelly.

'You're hateful,' Winnie told him with a scornful, dismissive jerk of her slight shoulders. 'I wouldn't marry you if you were the last man alive after an apocalypse! I have no respect for a man prepared to sink low enough to threaten my family while he tries to steal my son, and I wouldn't trust a word you said—'

'Teddy is my son and my family too,' Eros reasoned, lifting his strong chin. 'It is right that I do everything within my power—no matter how dirty I have to get—to do what I believe to be best for my son.'

Winnie had already retreated all the way back into the apartment. 'Well, just you keep on telling yourself that if it makes you feel better but, unlike

you, I have standards and rules I wouldn't break…
No—no matter what the temptation was!'

'You can't expect me to play nice in a situation
where you expect me to accept that my own child
will be perpetually out of my reach,' Eros argued
fiercely, green eyes snapping with intensity.

'When the dust settles,' Winnie responded curtly,
'just remember that *you* are the one who wanted
to make this a battle and fight dirty. *I* was the one
prepared to be reasonable and fair.'

'Really?' Eros slanted a scornful brow. 'Were
you fair when you concealed the birth of my child
from me? Were you fair when you denied Teddy
his right to have a father? Were you being fair
when you suggested that I could *maybe* arrange to
be in London more often to see my son?'

Her heart-shaped face tight and pale with angry
tension, Winnie screened her eyes and remained
silent, reluctant to engage in further argument with
him because it wasn't getting her anywhere. No,
none of that was fair. But it had not been any fairer
on her when Eros had concealed the reality that he
was a married man. It was, however, even more
unjust when he threatened to expose her sisters
in court as unsuitable carers for Teddy because of
past experiences that neither young woman could
have avoided or controlled.

Zoe had been bullied and abused in foster care.
Vivi had been left to take the fall for a wayward

young heiress from a powerful family. In short, life *wasn't* fair, Winnie conceded unhappily. She had first learned that when her loving, hardworking parents had died at the hands of a drunk driver and she had learned it afresh when she had trustingly given her heart to a man who had broken it.

But Eros wasn't going to get his hands on Teddy too, she swore vehemently to herself. She would fight back by appealing to her grandfather for help. The older man wanted her to marry some man of *his* choosing, so he would hardly support the idea of her marrying Eros, nor would he want Eros to have more power over his grandson than he had.

Indeed, so worked up was Winnie that she could not even wait until she got home to speak to Stam Fotakis. She phoned her grandfather on the way home and told him that Eros had demanded that she marry him.

'It's past time,' Stam commented, sending her reeling with that unforeseen response. 'But better late than never. He's the boy's father and when you marry him, my grandson gets his name and his birthright. Nevrakis isn't from an old family but he has good social standing and pots of money and at least he's not a spendthrift, womanising idiot like his late father...'

Winnie was gobsmacked by that reply enumerating Eros's advantages and it momentarily silenced her.

'Of course, you'll marry him. Why wouldn't you? He owes you a wedding ring,' her grandfather informed her sternly. 'It'll put *right* everything that was done wrong. Tell me the date and I'll even put in an appearance on the day.'

'I was planning to ask you to get me a good lawyer to fight him,' Winnie almost whispered, already reckoning that that was a hope doomed to failure.

'No, you'll have the benefit of my legal team when you're *divorcing* him,' Stam assured her with calm emphasis.

'But if I don't marry him, he's threatening to fight me for custody of Teddy.'

'But why wouldn't you want to marry him and put everything right?' the older man demanded in what sounded like honest disbelief. 'You said you would marry to please me.'

'Yes…anyone *but* Eros,' Winnie mumbled shakily.

'Nevrakis is my choice but don't worry, you and the little boy will be coming home with me after the wedding,' Stam informed her with immense satisfaction.

No way was he prepared to entrust Nevrakis with his granddaughter and great-grandson's future happiness, Stam reflected grimly. He would care for Winnie and Teddy, and give them the support and security that they needed to flourish. How could he possibly trust Nevrakis to do that for him? Neither respect nor care had featured in Nevrakis's behaviour during his affair with Winnie and Stam had never believed that a leopard could change his spots. Winnie and Teddy would be safer with him. It was his job to ensure that no further harm came to his family, so naturally they would have to leave Nevrakis and come home with Stam after the wedding. That was the only way that he could fully protect the pair of them from further harm.

It occurred to Winnie, even in her shell-shocked state of betrayal, that Eros wouldn't like getting married and then finding that his wife and child had flown, and she tottered into the house, only to be engulfed by her sisters and their frantic questions. For the first time ever, she found herself being less than honest with her siblings. How could she tell them that Eros had threatened to expose their secrets and frailties in an open courtroom? It would seriously distress and frighten them.

My goodness, had her grandfather engineered Eros's sudden reappearance in her life? What else was she to believe? Stam Fotakis was a control freak. He liked to pull strings, enjoyed manipulating people into doing his bidding. Was it her grandfather who had told Eros about Teddy? She should have worked out that reality from the minute Eros had appeared without warning, she censured herself severely. Where had her wits been when she'd accepted that that was only a coincidence? Combined with her grandfather's admission that he *wanted* her to marry Eros and Eros's sudden proposal, she felt as though she had been dangled like bait on a fish hook. What else didn't she know? What else had either man not told her? It infuriated her to be left in ignorance.

'Why the hell would you want to marry him?' Vivi demanded furiously.

Zoe cleared her throat. 'He's gorgeous, he's rich and she used to love him *and* he's Teddy's father. I disagree but I can understand where Grandad's coming from. Those inducements do provide quite a strong argument.'

'He's a rat!' Vivi objected.

'We also have John and Liz and Grandad's proposition to consider,' Winnie reminded her sisters quietly. 'He wants me to marry Eros and if I don't *have* to live with him, I think, I think I'll do it and that'll be that, *my* duty done.'

'But you *can't*,' Vivi argued emotively, her eyes full of compassion. 'Let's face it, you really don't want to be forced to have anything to do with Eros Nevrakis.'

'No, but beggars don't have choices,' Winnie breathed starkly. 'This is the price for my having made the mistake of having an affair with him. I'll do it for Teddy and for John and Liz.'

But she lay in bed that night thinking about

that kiss she had succumbed to, and hating herself like poison for still being that weak and vulnerable with a man who had almost destroyed her two years earlier. She had spent weeks locked in her bedroom before she had found employment, listening to songs of heartbreak on endless replay until the reality that she was pregnant and *had* to make plans for the future had finally pierced her shell of self-pity and made her pick herself up and shake herself down again.

A marriage that was only a marriage on paper to satisfy her grandfather would suit her to perfection. Eros wouldn't be able to threaten her or her sisters with her grandfather behind her as support, she told herself urgently. All she had to do was play along, let the arrangements take their course and wait for Eros to get stung in the tail by Stam Fotakis just as she and her sisters had been. Eros would not get her as a wife and he would not get Teddy either and, bearing in mind the way he had threatened her and Vivi *and* Zoe, that was exactly what he deserved… *Wasn't it?*

She had to look after Vivi and Zoe. Hadn't that always been her role as big sister? Yet her sisters had been separated from her as children and she had not been able to prevent them from suffering through unhappy and challenging experiences in foster care. That sad failure still on her conscience, Winnie knew that there was nothing she wouldn't do to protect her sisters' well-being now that they were adults.

And naturally she wanted nothing more to do with Eros, naturally she didn't want to live with the man! After all, he had pulled the wool over her eyes before and hurt her terribly. Obviously, she didn't want to give him another opportunity! Eros was her fatal flaw, her weakness. It was a shameful truth but there it was. She had no common sense around him and her defences were paper-thin. If she didn't guard herself, she would get hurt again and spending too much time exposed to Eros was an inexorable way of putting herself in jeopardy. She would just be an accident waiting to happen, she thought with a shiver of foreboding.

CHAPTER FIVE

Winnie would have been surprised to appreciate that her future husband on paper only was well aware of the size and calibre of the odds stacked up against him. Eros was shrewd and he already knew that his future grandfather-in-law loathed him for the sin of turning *his* granddaughter into an unmarried mother. Forewarned was forearmed as far as Eros was concerned and no sooner had Eros received a cool little phone call from Winnie informing him that she had thought the situation over and that she *would* marry him than he began putting in place the kind of security he had never dreamt he would have to hire.

Nevertheless, Stamboulas Fotakis was devious, and Eros had no intention of letting the older man control or manipulate him. Stam would have to be satisfied with having shocked Eros with the news that he was a father at their first meeting, for it was the only winning move he would get to make in the game unfolding. Eros would not allow either his wife or his child to be damaged by the conflict between himself and Teddy's great-grandfather. Stam would have to wise up and accept the status quo, Eros reflected grimly, determined to protect his future family from every malign influence, including that of an old man who was bitter and unforgiving.

While Eros was plotting with the same dexterity that his future grandfather-in-law excelled at, Winnie was shyly admitting that she was about to marry Teddy's father to John and Liz Brooke and receiving their entirely innocent approval and congratulations, for she had never told them that Eros had been a married man at the time of her son's conception. Vivi rolled her eyes in sympathy for that concealment of the unlovely truth and sat chatting to one of the teenage foster kids at the kitchen table while Zoe, as usual, busied herself round the kitchen as a background girl, hoping to deflect any interest anyone might have in her.

'I know it may seem old-fashioned for you young parents to get married these days but I'm very pleased,' Liz confided, squeezing Winnie's small hand, her plump face wreathed in a bright smile of pleasure. 'Marriage seems more secure to my generation. I wasn't criticising.'

'No, I know you weren't.' Winnie gave the older woman a hug while John, a quiet man at the best of times, beamed approval and mentioned that it would do Teddy good to have a father around.

The very first pang of guilt pierced Winnie at that moment because she knew she would be leaving Eros straight after the wedding to return to her grandfather's house. Teddy *wasn't* going to have a father around. Instead he would only enjoy occasional visits from him. Unfortunately for her, it went against her inherently honest nature to deceive anyone, *even* Eros. She knew that Eros was expecting her to stay with him, to act as a wife and a mother by his side, and the awareness of that lowering fact prevented her from experiencing even an ounce of satisfaction over the reality that she would be spiking Eros's big guns and threats with superior power.

Now, however, Winnie was finally looking beneath those superficial reactions and admitting a less welcome truth to herself. Frankly, she was terrified of the mere prospect of having to live with Eros, she admitted guiltily. In such a position she would end up letting her guard slip and she would let him hurt her all over again. In reality she was being a total coward about Eros because she was struggling to keep everyone else happy. She wanted to please her grandfather, save John and Liz and protect her siblings, and she could see no way other than marrying Eros to achieve those goals. What other option did she have?

So, of course, she was going to have to leave Eros after the wedding. That would make her grandfather and her sisters happy and it would also ensure that she didn't need to risk herself in Eros's radius again. It wouldn't make Eros happy, she acknowledged ruefully, but since she couldn't credit that he really wanted to marry her, she was convinced that he would soon see the benefits of almost immediately regaining his freedom.

Her grandfather phoned her when she returned home, telling her with positive good cheer that he had deposited sufficient funds in her bank account to cover what he called 'wedding fripperies.' 'All you have to do is buy your and your sisters' dresses. I will take care of everything else.'

In that assumption, however, Stamboulas Fotakis discovered himself to be sadly mistaken because Winnie's future husband informed him that the ceremony of marriage *had* to take place on the island of Trilis because it had been where his ancestors had married. Stam had never viewed Nevrakis as a sentimental man but on that one point the younger man was stubbornly immovable, and Stam knew that he could hardly refuse his future grandson-in-law the right to use the island and the house he had already promised him because it would be a sign of bad faith. Exasperated, Winnie's grandfather found himself having to adjust his plans to fit someone else's and it had been a very long time since Stam had suffered through that experience and bitten his tongue.

Perfectly conscious that he was creating waves, Eros flew out to Greece and organised a helicopter to take him out to the private island where no Nevrakis of his acquaintance had set foot in over thirty years. Even when his parents had still been together they had not visited the island because his father had very much preferred city life. The house had been renovated in the eighties, presumably sometime after Winnie's grandfather had acquired ownership, and since then it had been maintained in pristine condition, so, on that score, Eros had no complaints. The property was fully fit for occupation and for wedding catering.

Eros stood on the cliff gazing out to sea, enjoying the sunlight slowly tapering into a peach-coloured sunset while he thought with satisfaction about showing that same view to his son and to his wife. He was certain that Winnie had absolutely no idea of her grandfather's intention of stealing her and Teddy back on their wedding day. Unfortunately for Fotakis, the minute he had gone into a rant at their first meeting, insisting that neither Winnie nor Teddy actually *needed* Eros in their lives, Eros had smelled a rat and acted accordingly.

Where Winnie was concerned, however, he was convinced that she did not have a single sly, cheating bone in her little curvy body. That was, after all, what had first attracted him to her, he freely acknowledged.

He could read her expressive face like a picture book. She scored low in the feminine guile and calculation stakes and she didn't play power games like her grandfather or like many of the women Eros had met in his thirty years. No, what you saw was what you got with Winnie, unlike her grandfather, prepared to pressure a bridegroom into a wedding that he had no intention of allowing to become a marriage. Stam, however, was known for having done something similar with his eldest son, refusing to accept the wife his son had chosen and eventually becoming estranged from his own flesh and blood over his choice of partner. It was a track record that telegraphed a loud warning to Eros that he was dealing with a man who only ever paid heed to his own feelings and beliefs. He had displayed sufficient antipathy for Eros to recognise that the older man would not willingly accept him as a member of his family circle.

Winnie and her sisters went shopping. Neither Vivi nor Zoe paid the smallest heed to Winnie's plea to keep expenses to the minimum. In fact even Zoe laughed at that suggestion, reminding Winnie that it was to be a society wedding and the last thing Stam Fotakis would want was his grandchild dressed like a bargain-basement bride. Even Winnie, nonetheless, was overwhelmed by the whole bridal-salon experience and the kind of feminine extras that there had never before been room for in her budget.

Eros phoned her around noon and Zoe answered Winnie's phone because Winnie was being eased into a foaming mass of lace by two assistants.

'It's Eros…' she said, extending the phone once Winnie had emerged again.

'Lunch?' Eros enquired.

'Er…' Tumbled and flushed, Winnie stared at herself in the full-length mirror and knew she still hadn't found the right dress because it was too fussy and frilly for her taste. 'I'm trying on wedding stuff,' she muttered. 'Today's not good.'

'Dinner tonight, then,' Eros decided arrogantly.

'No, I—' Winnie began, keen to avoid him as much as was humanly possible.

'I haven't seen you since you agreed to marry me,' Eros reminded her darkly. 'Is there a reason for that?'

Something like panic infiltrated Winnie and she dragged in a stark breath, reminding herself that she had to play along and that avoiding him altogether wasn't an option. 'No, tonight will do fine. What time?'

Zoe dropped the phone back into Winnie's bag and looked at her expectantly.

'Dinner tonight,' she muttered in explanation.

'Put on your acting shoes,' Vivi advised. 'Of

course, he's going to expect to see you and discuss arrangements and the like.'

'I suppose,' Winnie mumbled grudgingly.

'Not that dress. Makes you look like a dumpy version of a ballerina doll,' Vivi whispered, making her older sister loose an involuntary giggle.

Even so, Winnie found it a challenge to regain her former light-hearted mood and reminded herself that it scarcely mattered what she wore to a fake wedding. But she chose a gown she liked, a sleek elegant dress that did wonders for her small curvy figure, reasoning that she needed to look her best with so many guests being invited by her grandfather and Eros.

She borrowed a dress and shoes from Zoe to wear that evening. Her own wardrobe was small and contained few smart outfits. The dress was black and unremarkable in every way, which suited her attitude to dining out with Eros.

'It's a funeral dress,' Vivi scolded. 'It's long and it's shapeless—'

'And it will do fine,' Winnie cut in impatiently.

'Don't mind me,' Vivi said drily. 'But you're supposed to be playing the happy bride-to-be.'

'I'm not happy about any of this,' Winnie admitted ruefully.

'That man is about to get exactly what he deserves!' Vivi proclaimed vengefully.

'Two wrongs don't make a right,' Zoe reasoned

with a wince, squeezing Winnie's hand in sympathy. 'Maybe you'll decide to give him another chance… Who knows?'

'Get a life, Zoe!' Vivi exclaimed. 'Eros wants his son, *not* Winnie.'

Winnie's slight shoulders hunched and colour faded from her cheeks. That even her sisters saw that so clearly mortified her.

'I'm sorry,' Vivi muttered ruefully to her older sister. 'But what else are we supposed to think? He's divorced but he didn't come looking for you even when he was free, *did he*?'

'No,' Winnie conceded, sucking in a steadying breath when faced with that truth again, hating herself for squirming at the reminder. What did it matter with only a fake wedding ahead of her? What did *any* of it matter now? She had loved him but *he* hadn't loved her, the oldest story of heartbreak in the world and one of the most common, she told herself impatiently.

'Maybe he felt guilty too,' Zoe muttered. 'Maybe he didn't feel entitled to be happy after his divorce.'

'Oh…*you*!' Vivi scolded her optimistic kid sister. 'You'd find a bright side to any catastrophe!'

None of those somewhat distressing conversations put Winnie in the mood to see Eros again. She reckoned she was oversensitive to the pain that Eros had caused her and equally thin-skinned when it came to that past being discussed because he had been a subject her siblings had staunchly avoided during the period when she was nursing a broken heart. Fortunately, she had moved on, got over him, *completely* got over him, she reminded herself doggedly.

It didn't help to walk out to the limousine that was there to collect her and see Eros standing beside the open passenger door in dialogue with a man who was unmistakeably one of her grandfather's security team. One glance at that classic bronzed profile and the sheer height and elegance of him in a formal dinner jacket and narrow black trousers and she was challenged to even swallow.

Her heart started thumping very fast inside her, a memory stirring of Eros arriving late at the country house one Friday evening, having attended a banking dinner he couldn't avoid. Heat washed up over her dismayed face and she ducked past Eros and darted straight into the limo, only unfortunately nothing could drown out her recollection of having had mad passionate sex on the sofa in the drawing room with him that night. She had been shocked by how desperate he had seemed for her and then foolishly pleased, deeming it a sign of deeper attachment. She hated looking back with hindsight, seeing how stupid she had been, continually mistaking sex for love.

'What's wrong?' Eros asked, studying her rigidity.

'Nothing's wrong!' Winnie proclaimed, dry-mouthed with tension, thinking wildly of an excuse to explain her discomfiture. 'It's all the wedding stuff…such a fuss. I can't think straight.'

'I thought all women enjoyed that sort of thing,' Eros admitted.

'Me…not so much,' she said truthfully, even knowing that once, had it been a real, *proper* wedding backed by love and need, she would have been overjoyed to be marrying him. That time was past, gone, she recalled, furious with herself for even *thinking* along those lines.

'It won't last long,' Eros said soothingly, trying not to remember the planning insanity of his first wedding. 'We're getting married the middle of next week on Trilis.'

'Trilis? Where's that?'

'A private island in Greece where the Nevrakis family started out as olive farmers and also ran a small hotel.'

'I assumed I'd be getting married at Grandad's house.'

'My family always get married on the island,' Eros countered smoothly.

Winnie swallowed hard on the objections brimming on her lips, wondering how much harder it would be to leave an island after the public wedding

show was over. She had no doubt that her grandfather had already factored in that added difficulty
to his plans because he was not a man to leave anything undone. But guilt gnawed at Winnie's conscience because Eros was taking the wedding as
seriously as though he were a real bridegroom…

My family always get married on the island.

She wondered if he had married his first wife
there and then punished herself for that inappropriate piece of curiosity by reminding herself of
how he had threatened to harm her entirely innocent sisters. Eros Nevrakis did not deserve her
guilt, she told herself urgently. He was as ruthless as a killing machine in shark form, taking
what he wanted without care for what it might
cost someone else.

Stam Fotakis had already helped her and her
sisters a great deal and she owed the older man
not just gratitude but loyalty, she reminded herself
firmly. She had to choose sides, there was no other
option and every instinct warned her to choose her
family and put them first. Perhaps then she could
pursue her dream of establishing a closer relationship with her grandad.

Eros took her, not to his apartment, which relieved her, but to an exclusive club where they
were seated in a very private velvet-lined booth
that was screened-off from the crowd. She had noticed the attention he received on arrival, the subtle

straightening, turning of heads that all signalled the arrival of an envied, highly attractive and very wealthy alpha male. Female heads turned even faster and lingered on Eros, glancing at her, brows lifting because she didn't look glamorous enough to fit the expected mould. People were probably wondering if she was a niece or the daughter of a friend or even an employee.

After what had felt like a very public entrance, the booth felt *too* cosy and *he* felt too close, her spine tingling at the dark timbre of his accented drawl, gooseflesh rippling across her skin when he carelessly brushed her hand with his as he passed her the menu. Iridescent sea-glass eyes enhanced by lush black lashes surveyed her levelly from across the table, his lean, dark, classically handsome features so strikingly flawless that, for a split second, she couldn't rip her attention from his spectacular bone structure.

His obvious relaxation taunted her simmering tension. Winnie could feel every breath she drew along with the wanton tightening of her nipples and the lick of pulsing heat curling between her thighs. It was unnerving that he could still awaken those responses in her treacherous body and it made her hate him more than ever for destroying the idealistic, romantic innocence that had been hers before she met him.

'You're incredibly quiet tonight,' Eros remarked lazily. 'I used to like that about you.'

'But a quiet woman is less of a challenge.'

'By the time I met you I had had enough of being challenged,' Eros admitted, lashes dipping, evading her scrutiny as if he already feared that he had revealed too much.

Challenged by his wife? Possibly Tasha had discovered his infidelity, although she had not appeared remotely suspicious of Winnie when she'd arrived at the country house and Winnie had behaved like an employee for Tasha's benefit for the first time in weeks. She had made a meal for his wife and it had hurt her pride to play the servant, driving home the lesson of how very foolish she had been to get into bed with a man whom she knew next to nothing about. It hadn't helped either to see a wife very much more beautiful than she was herself. Tasha was a sleek, shapely blonde with lively blue eyes and a pronounced air of energy, chattering into her phone constantly to rap out instructions to an employee and answer queries in a variety of languages. Beautiful, accomplished and confident, everything Winnie was not.

Winnie had packed and left that house and her job that same day, filled with shame and regret. Memories could be so cruel, she registered abruptly, realising that she had carried that demeaning sense of being less and second best ever since that humiliating day.

'We will make this marriage work,' Eros told her arrogantly over the first course of the meal. 'It *has* to work for Teddy.'

Chilled inside by that insistent statement, Winnie toyed with her food, thinking about Teddy, who was perfectly happy with his mother and his aunts. *But for how long will that phase of his childhood last?* a little voice prompted her for the first time. Children grew up fast and developed more complex needs. Eros would still have visiting rights though, and Teddy would learn to value his father and divide his loyalties as all children of parents who lived apart had to do. He would be fine, absolutely fine, she told herself bracingly.

'This is very important to me,' Eros intoned in the smouldering silence. 'Why do I get the impression that you're not even listening?'

Winnie faked a yawn with her hand. 'I'm sorry. I'm very tired.'

It would be the first time a woman had fallen asleep on him, Eros reflected grimly, exasperated by her silence, her seeming refusal to make the smallest effort. What was the matter with her? This was *not* Winnie as he recalled her, but then she had walked out on him, become a mother alone, struggled to survive and the experience was bound to have changed her. Yet if they were to stay together, they had to find a bridge between the past and the present. Sex? He knew he couldn't wait to have her under him again, over him, in front of him…just about any way he could have her.

No, *that* hadn't changed, he acknowledged reluctantly, that raw driving hunger to possess that she incited and which he had never understood or accepted. It had hurt his pride, it had exasperated him with *her*, with *himself* because he distrusted anything he couldn't control and he *hadn't* been able to control the fierce need she provoked. Yet he had repeatedly tried to explain it to himself, talk himself out of those urges, constantly challenging himself with self-denial while he fought to get his discipline back.

Unarguably, however, the truth remained that Winnie sat there in an ugly cloaking black dress that revealed nothing of her very sensual curves and with only the smallest encouragement he would *still* have spread her across the table and fallen on her like a sex-starved animal.

CHAPTER SIX

'YOU LOOK AMAZING!' Vivi sighed as Winnie performed a twirl in front of the built-in cheval mirror on the wall of the luxury cabin.

It was a beautiful dress, fashioned of Venice lace and organza, cut to fit Winnie's shapely figure like a glove. An enticing row of pearl buttons ran down her spine to her hip. The sweetheart neckline emphasised her sister's curves while the mermaid style flared out from her knees with very real elegance and not with the kind of fullness of fabric that would have accentuated Winnie's diminutive height.

'We all do but, like all brides, Winnie takes the crown,' Zoe murmured fondly. 'I feel like pinching myself to see if this is real. Here we are on a fabulous yacht, cruising to our sister's wedding on a private island… It's like a dream or like suddenly being plunged into a movie.'

'I wonder if you'll feel quite so chirpy when it's *your* wedding day,' Vivi remarked with an edge of warning.

'But we don't have to worry about that. Grandad is going to whisk us all away again before we need to worry about consequences.' Zoe's bright confidence in Stamboulas Fotakis's ability to work miracles was unconcealed. 'Eros wanted to transport all of us to the island because he made the island a no-fly zone to keep the paparazzi from buzzing the wedding from above,' she reminded her siblings. 'And Grandad got around that change of plan by borrowing a pal's massive yacht for the occasion.'

'Yes, Grandad's pretty wily,' Winnie agreed, still studying her reflection, her heart beating so fast with nerves it felt as though it were thumping through her entire body like a ticking time bomb on countdown.

'Pittee,' Teddy told her, yanking on her gown for attention.

'*Pretty?* That's a new word. Wonder where he picked up that one,' Vivi commented, snatching her nephew up into a hug. 'No, you're not allowed to touch Mama's dress with those little hands, but I'm wearing black, so you can do all the grabbing you want round Aunt Zoe and me!'

Teddy giggled with delight as Vivi turned him upside down, swung him round and dumped him on the massive bed for a spot of tickling and the sort of rough play he adored. Winnie paced anxiously. Eros had visited them in London twice to see Teddy but Winnie hadn't seen him since that tense and disturbing evening meal they had shared. She had been at work, for, although her grandfather and Eros had both scoffed at the idea of such dutiful behaviour, Winnie had worked out her notice, giving the restaurant owner time to find and engage her replacement.

The yacht was slowing down radically to enter the harbour and dock. When they disembarked they were heading straight to the church before moving up to the Nevrakis house on the hill for the reception. When it came to making the return trip to Athens, both Winnie and her sisters already had their instructions. All they had to do was slip away and walk back down to the little harbour, where the yacht would await their arrival. Teddy would be brought there in a separate manoeuvre. 'Why not leave straight after the church ceremony?' she had asked her grandfather. 'Surely that would be easier.'

His answer had disturbed her.

'I want my guests and his to see Nevrakis dance to my tune and then become the abandoned bridegroom on his wedding day,' Stamboulas Fotakis had assured her with satisfaction.

Winnie had paled and instantly felt queasy because, strange as it might seem, that aspect of her grandfather's plans hadn't occurred to her. Worrying about how she and her son might get away again had consumed her and she had never paused to stop and think about what her unexpected vanishing act would actually mean to Eros or how it would affect him, beyond angering him, of course. And somehow, she didn't know why, the concept of humiliating Eros in front of a crowd made her feel quite sick and ashamed. That kind of revenge wasn't her style even if it was her aggressive grandad's. She didn't want to *hurt* Eros because he was her son's father and insulting and injuring him could only damage an already strained relationship. Why hadn't she thought of that issue sooner? Now it was too late, she conceded unhappily, hurriedly reminding herself of how ruthless Eros had been when he'd threatened her vulnerable sisters. Eros could look after himself perfectly well, she reasoned feverishly.

He wouldn't walk away from Teddy but he would realise he had lost any power over her and her siblings. That was how it *had* to be. She didn't have a choice just as her sisters didn't have a choice. This was the price of saving the roof over their foster parents' heads. Goodness knew, after all the good John and Liz had done for Winnie, Vivi and Zoe and so many other troubled and unhappy teenagers, the older couple deserved the sisters' protection and the security of no longer having to fear the loss of their home. Even so, she was sad that she was getting married without the older couple's presence and knew they had been disappointed. Unfortunately, not only would it have been very hard for either John or Liz to leave their foster children for a couple of days with their busy schedule, but also she couldn't possibly tell them the truth, that it *wasn't* a real or normal wedding. Saving John and Liz had entailed a lot of fibs and half-truths that still sat on Winnie's conscience like lead weights.

'It's time.' Their grandfather lodged in the doorway, ultrasmart in his tailored morning suit and cravat. 'You look delightful, Winnie. Nevrakis will be disappointed when he realises that he doesn't get to keep you or my great-grandson.'

Oxygen rattled in Winnie's tight throat. 'Eros is tough. He'll get over it,' she said flatly, thinking of the man who had moved on untouched by their broken relationship and the hurt inflicted on her. 'He's one of life's survivors.'

'As are you,' Vivi reminded her as they walked out onto the deck and began the delicate operation of getting the bride off the yacht without brushing her gown against anything that could mark its pristine ivory threaded with gold folds.

Two classic cars bedecked with flowers awaited them at the harbour and a sizeable crowd provided an audience. Winnie accompanied her grandfather into the first, her sisters and her son entered the second. Her chest tight as a drum with tension, she struggled to smile like a bride when her grandfather urged her. Every floral tribute she saw, every well-wisher reminded her that she was taking part in an unsavoury plan. The cars ferried them only a couple of hundred yards to a picturesque little stone church overlooking the sea with a little village full of white-painted houses climbing the hill behind it.

'There won't be many witnesses to the ceremony in a place this small,' Stam Fotakis lamented at her side, but his granddaughter was relieved by the same fact.

John and Liz took their foster kids to church but pressured no one who preferred not to go. Winnie discovered a new fear bubbling up in her chest, the fear that she was enacting a heavenly punishable offence in undergoing a wedding ceremony without the intent of following through. A civil ceremony would have been preferable, she brooded uncomfortably. A squad of people waited outside the church to witness the bride's arrival, calling out greetings and good wishes. With her sisters beside her, however, she felt stronger and less oversensitive.

Inside the dim old church with its candles, painted murals of the saints and beautiful white floral displays, her focus leapt straight to the man at the foot of the aisle. Eros turned round, his classic bronzed profile alert to her arrival. Beneath her gown, she could feel her entire body heat and flush with awareness. His brilliant green eyes were gilded in the candlelit interior and her mouth ran dry. Even the morning suit that made her grandad look a little rotund and small could only embellish Eros's all-male beauty, showcasing every lithe athletic inch of his broad-shouldered, lean-hipped, long-legged length.

'Gorgeous dress,' he muttered half under his breath as they both turned to face the Greek Orthodox priest.

Finding her breath in the ritual that followed, bearing up to the crushing solemnity of the occasion in which she understood only sporadic words were a challenge for her. Eros slid the ring, an elaborate engraved platinum circle, onto her finger and she breathed again because it was done. She was the wife of the man she had once loved to the edge of insanity and her eyes stung with a sudden rush of moisture because the wounding memories seemed very close to the surface at that moment and she welcomed those thoughts, needing the armour of her hatred for him to defend her from other feelings and sensations.

'Papa!' Teddy shook free of Zoe's hand and pounced on Eros as they moved down the aisle again.

That word, that very designation, being openly awarded to Eros shook Winnie up. When had *that* started? Why had nobody warned her? Of course, it was reality, she reminded herself soothingly, and not all the wishing in the world could change it. Even before the wedding she had been tied for life by her son to a man she despised. An unscrupulous guy without principles, who took what he wanted when he wanted without regard for the consequences to anyone else. For all she knew, she brooded, his wife had divorced him for his infidelity and if he hadn't been faithful to Tasha, he wouldn't be planning to be any more faithful to his second wife, for cheaters were known to repeat their habits.

Those grim ruminations rebuilt her defences and bolstered her strength to face the walkout she had to stage. Eros might be Teddy's *papa* but he was *not* a nice guy, not a man in need of her sympathy or guilty conscience, she told herself urgently.

While unaware of his bride's dark thoughts, Eros, nonetheless, read her tension and assumed it was caused by her shy dislike of being the centre of attention. That was so very different from his first wedding that there was no comparison to be made and he was relieved by that acknowledgement. He had never seen the point of bestowing blame on either himself or Tasha for a marriage breakdown that had seemed inevitable to him from the very first day of their convenient arrangement.

He had done his best to uphold their paper marriage. He had done his duty for years, struggling not to be selfish, struggling to be fair and honourable even when it had become an almighty challenge and their marriage had been in name only. That he had finally failed was something he no longer held against himself as he had once done. Nobody was perfect, neither him nor anyone else. All that troubled him in the present was that Winnie had somehow ended up paying the ultimate cost for his failure. For that same reason he could tolerate Stam Fotakis's loathing with calm control because, in the old man's shoes, he knew that he might well have felt the same.

Winnie settled back into the classic car while Teddy, who complained hugely, was strapped into a car seat. 'You thought of everything,' she remarked in surprise at the presence of the seat.

'Obviously we would want Teddy with us,' Eros parried.

As the car climbed the steep driveway that wound up past the little village, Winnie craned her neck, curious to see the Nevrakis home. 'For how long have your family lived here?'

Eros saw no reason to tell Winnie that he had only reclaimed the island by marrying her. What would be the point? It would only make her more suspicious than ever about his motives, he reasoned impatiently. In time she would learn that fact and he would deal with it then.

'The first house was a farmhouse owned by my great-grandfather, the olive farmer, who turned it into a small hotel. My grandfather razed that building to the ground and rebuilt and in due course, when he died, my father did the same even though he had no intention of ever making this his permanent home.'

Winnie's brows lifted in bewilderment. 'No intention? Then why on earth would he—'

'I think a weird mixture of family pride and his innate streak of extravagance persuaded him into wasting his inheritance here even though he found island life boring. Although Trilis is quite a reasonable size, it couldn't possibly offer him the social life he enjoyed in Athens.'

'So, you didn't grow up here on the island?' Winnie asked, determined to satisfy her curiosity now that Eros was finally answering her questions.

'No, I grew up in an Athens apartment, almost exclusively with my mother. She's gone now too,' Eros confided flatly. 'So are my grandparents on both sides. There is only me and Teddy and now you in the Nevrakis family. There are a few distant cousins attending the reception but no close relations. I'm surprised you didn't invite your foster parents.'

Winnie went pink and trotted out her excuses about how difficult it was for either John or Liz to leave home even for a short time. 'As foster carers they have constant meetings with social workers, schools, birth parents.'

An ebony brow slanted up. 'Still, you were very fond of them as I recall and I'm sure they would've made a special effort.'

'I didn't want to put them under that pressure,' Winnie muttered in desperation. 'John's health can be dicey.'

It was a relief to step out into the sunlight again and see her sisters emerging from the car behind. They all stared at the house, which she thought was stupendously large for a property in which Eros's father had apparently not planned to live. Extravagant, Eros had labelled his father, and Winnie was inclined to agree as they entered a grand marble-floored hall to be greeted by staff offering drinks on silver trays.

Her grandfather strolled to her side. 'It is done,' he pronounced with satisfaction. 'The ring you deserve is on your finger now.'

Winnie looked down at her finger uncomfortably just as Eros stretched out a hand to her, obviously keen to introduce her to some of the guests arriving. The next hour and more passed in a whirl of introductions and harmless chatter, by which time Teddy was flagging, hungry and overtired.

'I took the liberty of bringing in a nanny for the day,' Eros murmured, disconcerting his bride. 'Teddy can have an early lunch and a nap to recoup his energies while the adults celebrate.'

Winnie could not argue with such a sensible suggestion and the warm, friendly woman who approached with a ready smile was very different from the coldly efficient carer Eros had hired in London for the zoo trip. Agathe swiftly gained her son's trust and, with his aunt Zoe's comforting presence secured as well, Teddy had no objection to being carried off upstairs.

In the doorway of a vast pillared ballroom full of tables and chairs for the reception, Winnie paused and swallowed her surprise. 'I expected a canvas marquee in the garden,' she admitted.

'No, my father covered even the most remote possibilities when he built this place,' Eros confided with rueful amusement. 'And perhaps you can also see why he eventually ended up bankrupt.'

As they were escorted to the top table, Winnie scanned the fabulous view of the sea and the island from the house's splendid clifftop location. A wall of glass ran down one side of the ballroom, multiple doors opening out onto a furnished terrace. Her curious gaze lingered on the borrowed yacht dominating the little harbour and she paled, losing her focus again. Soon, *soon*, she reminded herself, she would be sailing away with Teddy and her sisters and this nightmare wedding would simply be like something from a bad dream that she would never have to think about again.

Long brown fingers feathered down her rigid spine and her entire body tingled, locked into sudden instinctive craving. She glanced up at Eros from beneath her feathery lashes and, with a husky growl deep in his throat, he reached for her, taking her so much by surprise that she simply froze, locked into place like a statue.

His firm, yet soft lips forced hers apart and his tongue delved and she shook and shivered as a gathering storm of sensation bombarded her. In all her life she had never wanted anything as much as she wanted Eros at that moment. A piercing dart of feverish longing shot from low in her body, rousing sweet tingling heat, clenching the muscles in her pelvis so tight she gasped, even more painfully aware of the response between her thighs.

'*Thee mou*... I want you,' Eros muttered roughly into her hair as he jerked his mouth off hers again as though he had been burned.

And in a way, they had *both* been burned, Winnie acknowledged feverishly, conscious of the tiny tremors racking the lean, powerful body melded to hers and the thrusting proof of his arousal. She still wanted him; it made her hate herself but Winnie had never been the sort to deny an obvious truth. The same passionate attraction that had blindsided them the first time around hadn't died and hadn't been conquered by common sense or pride or even guilt. She was ashamed of it, ashamed of the shake in her hand as she used the table to steady herself on locked knees that still trembled. It was a moment when she was almost grateful for the reminder of how much power Eros could still have over her and how very dangerous he could be to her peace of mind. *Been there, done that, got Teddy... Never again*, she told herself with finality.

'Your nerves are showing,' Vivi whispered under cover of releasing her sister's gown from where it had caught on her high-heeled sandal.

Winnie compressed her lips. 'I'm no good at faking it,' she admitted.

'Good news on my wedding night,' Eros murmured sibilantly, lean hands splaying possessively across her hips from behind, the combination of both voice and touch very nearly inducing a panic attack in Winnie as her triangular face flared hotter than hellfire.

Winnie barely touched the meal set in front of her. She nudged stuff round the plate, trying to conceal her lack of appetite. She listened to the world-famous harpist playing atmospheric Greek folk songs, tapped her foot with determination when livelier music followed and only tensed when her grandfather caught her eye with a faint tilt of his chin. Almost as quickly her sisters were approaching her, talking about needing to straighten her hair and, without hesitation, she slid out of her seat and followed them out of the reception to the palatial cloakroom.

'There's a car waiting at the back entrance. All

you have to do is walk out across the courtyard garden,' Vivi began tautly.

'I can't leave without Teddy!' Winnie gasped in consternation.

'Grandad's men are fetching Teddy,' Zoe told her soothingly. 'We only have to get down to the harbour.'

Winnie didn't feel comfortable walking out of a house where her son slept upstairs, unaware of his family's departure but her sisters were as nervous as she was, and nerves made the two younger women assertive, thrusting her through the French windows into the fresh air, both of them catching onto her wrists, urging her in the right direction, giving her no chance to change her mind.

'This doesn't feel right,' she protested in the courtyard garden, a sunny tranquil space that mocked the drama being enacted.

'We need to get out of here...*fast*!' Vivi exclaimed impatiently, pushing her sister through the gate into the rear lane where an SUV idled its engine in readiness.

Having been alerted by the security team he had engaged, Eros observed their departure from the same rear hallway. A kind of white-hot rage unlike anything he had ever felt before surged through him when he saw Winnie pass through the last barrier in the direction of the waiting car.

His wife walking out on him.

Nothing could've prepared him for that view. Nothing until that instant could've persuaded him that Winnie would do anything so dishonest as to enter a church with him, speak marital vows and then take off like a bat out of hell afterwards. But there she was, the living proof of his delusional belief that she was *different* from the other women he had known. And the truth was that she wasn't one bit different from her predecessors, who had convinced him that women were in no way the more delicate, honest and reliable sex, he derided grimly. In fact, she was one of the worst deceivers and the biggest fraud.

Winnie was shaking like a leaf by the time she finally boarded the yacht, perspiration marking her brow, eyes wide with apprehension, her heart pounding fit to burst. Her grandfather's cheerful greeting made her turn angrily away. 'Teddy?' she began anxiously.

'Teddy will be here in approximately thirty seconds,' Stamboulas Fotakis assured her confidently.

But the car that drove down to the harbour was not the one the older man was apparently expecting. It was a sports car, with a child seat fitted, driven by Eros. He climbed out, whisked his sobbing son from the seat into his arms and lounged back against the bonnet of the sports car cradling the little boy with supreme cool.

'Oh, dear heaven…' Winnie whispered, dry-mouthed. 'Eros *knows*.'

Her grandfather said something very rude in Greek about Eros's ancestors.

'I can't leave,' Winnie breathed shakily. 'There's no way I can leave Teddy here.'

'Don't be ridiculous. We'll come back for him. Nevrakis can't guard him 24/7,' Stam Fotakis growled. 'Nor can he keep him from his mother.'

But Winnie was unconvinced. She studied Eros, the man she had married mere hours earlier. She didn't need to speak to him to understand exactly what he was telling her. His message was etched in the slumberous relaxation of his lean, power-ful physique as he leant back against the car and in the steady direction of his gaze. He had Teddy, and in their son he held *all* the cards that could possibly be played.

'Winnie…' Her grandfather rested a heavy hand on her rigid shoulder. 'Listen to me.'

'No,' she said curtly. 'Listening to you is where I went wrong. If I don't go back, Eros will fight tooth and nail to keep Teddy and I will *not* risk losing my son.'

'I won't let him do that.'

'He's already outwitted you and you hate him. I can't trust your promises when it comes to the well-being of the most important person in my life,' Winnie muttered shakily, stepping back from her siblings' attempts to offer her sympathy. 'I'm going back.'

'But you *can't*!' Vivi exclaimed. 'You didn't sign up for that!'

'Winnie *has* to go back for Teddy. What else can she do now?' Zoe groaned.

Winnie watched Eros straighten as she climbed back down into the tender that would whisk her back to shore. She watched him smile with satisfaction, the fierce gratified smile of a man who knew he had won the most important game he would ever play. It was a game very much centred on family.

She had played the same game and lost, alongside her grandfather, she acknowledged between gritted teeth, ready to spontaneously combust with anger, resentment and anxiety about the kind of welcome that awaited her on shore.

CHAPTER SEVEN

ANOTHER CAR DREW up at the harbour and Winnie waited while the car seat was installed, freezing into stillness as Eros approached her and extended Teddy, who was sleepily snuffling and tear-stained. Her husband's silence unnerved her as much as the chill in the emerald-green eyes welded to her flushed and discomfited face. Eros turned the sports car and drove off ahead of them, her transport whisking her at a more sedate pace back up to the house on the hill and the reception she had vacated in such a panic. Still half-asleep, Teddy clung to her.

Emerging from the vehicle, Winnie stilled and bit at the soft underside of her lower lip. 'What now?' she whispered unevenly as Eros stalked up to her.

Eros's brilliant gaze flashed like a storm warning between lush black lashes. '*Now* we entertain our guests until their departure. Luckily for us, your grandfather is not known for his company manners. That he left early with your sisters will not surprise anyone. You went down to the harbour merely to say goodbye to your family.'

His icy intonation had scoured every scrap of colour from Winnie's cheeks. 'We have to talk.'

'*After* the wedding,' Eros traded with sardonic emphasis. 'I refuse to parade my mistakes in front of an audience.'

Her teeth clenched so tightly at his ready admission that marrying her had been a mistake that she hurt her gums. Even so, she swallowed hard on an acid retort because, whether she liked it or not, discretion made better sense, particularly when it would protect Teddy from witnessing the conflict between his parents.

What remained of the afternoon and early evening felt unbearably long and was an unimaginable strain for Winnie. Her jaw ached from smiling and with the amount of effort required to keep Teddy entertained and in a good mood. It felt like a relief to pop her son into a bath after a quick supper and then hand him over to the hovering nanny until it occurred to her that she still had to face Eros.

For a bridegroom, Eros had contrived to give her a very wide berth since their return to the reception and when one of the guests had expressed surprise at the newly married couple's failure to take to the dance floor, Eros had smoothly concocted the excuse that his bride was suffering from a recently sprained ankle that was still tender.

Yes, Winnie was learning all sorts of unwelcome facts about the man she had married, facts that were distinctly unsettling. Eros was outrageously nimble and versatile in a tight corner and a far better dissembler than her grandfather, who had struggled to conceal his hostility throughout the wedding. With Machiavellian cunning, Eros had masked his suspicions yet still contrived to coolly outmanoeuvre the older man. Eros had played them all, she recognised angrily, let her make an absolute fool of herself traipsing down to the harbour while knowing from the outset that as long as he retained physical possession of their son, *she* was unlikely to leave. Eros had won by using Teddy as a weapon and that infuriated her.

As she hovered in the doorway of the fully furnished nursery, listening to Teddy's drowsy little snuffles as he drifted off to sleep, Eros materialised by her side. She hadn't heard his approach and she flinched back a step.

'Let's go downstairs,' he suggested, his tone perfectly pleasant and in no way threatening.

But Winnie wasn't hoodwinked because she gazed up into that lean, darkly handsome face and collided with green sea-glass eyes as cool and cutting as ice shards and her tummy turned over sickly as if she were falling from a great height.

'I've dismissed the staff for the night,' Eros volunteered. 'They'll clean up tomorrow. The nanny, Agathe, will be staying, however, for Teddy's benefit.'

'I am capable of looking after my son on my own,' Winnie framed curtly.

'Are you?' Eros sounded dubious on that score.

Determined to retain her temper, Winnie compressed her generous mouth as she traversed the stairs ahead of him.

'After all,' Eros continued, refined as a polished steel rapier in her wake, 'you were ready to sacrifice my relationship with Teddy, regardless of how losing his father would affect him.'

'No, I wasn't. You would still have had access to him whenever you wanted!' Winnie argued vehemently as she whirled round in the echoing hall, which was far too grand in size and space for comfort.

His beautiful shapely mouth curled in disagreement. 'Not if your grandfather had anything to do with it. I think we both know that Stam had every intention of writing me back *out* of Teddy's life!'

'That may be true but *I'm* Teddy's parent and I wouldn't have allowed that to happen,' Winnie claimed with spirit, too overwrought to stand still and walking restively through the huge reception room ahead, which was still littered with glasses. Indeed with all the debris from the wedding reception, it made her think of a ghost ship abandoned by its crew.

'Thankfully you are no longer Teddy's *sole* parent,' Eros ground out with grim emphasis, watching her cross the ballroom at speed to head through the nearest doors onto the terrace outside. For Eros it was like being brought back to the scene of the crime…an unwelcome reminder of the wedding that hadn't really been a wedding and the blushing bride, who had never intended to be a bride. His temper was as raw-edged as the sharpest knife. 'Now you have to share that responsibility with me.'

'I don't intend to share anything with you!' Winnie flung back at him over her shoulder as she reached the fresh air and drank it in deep, struggling to control the nerves flashing through her and the confused emotions bombarding her. She would not allow Eros to make her feel ashamed of what she had done, she swore to herself. Sometimes life enforced unpleasant choices and she had done the best she could with poor prospects.

'But you're stuck here now,' Eros pointed out softly, even while his dark deep drawl vibrated in the smouldering silence. 'And you will *not* leave this island or take Teddy from it until I am satisfied that I can *trust* you.'

So shocked was Winnie by that provocative threat that she spun round to face him again, brown eyes huge with disbelief in her expressive face, her chest heaving.

For an instant, Eros found his concentration slipping. Even in a rage, he was still a man and the heave of Winnie's luscious lace-covered breasts was as eye-catching as it was arousing. It also brought to mind the lowering awareness that this was not how he had expected to spend his wedding night. But then how would he know what was normal on a wedding night? he asked himself sardonically. He had never had a normal marriage and now it looked as if history was set on cruel repeat, a possibility he absolutely refused to accept a second time around.

Either he was married or he wasn't. There would be no halfway deal, no unreasonable conditions set between him and Winnie. Yet at the same time he refused to contemplate another divorce. They had to put Teddy first and, as far as he was concerned, putting Teddy first entailed giving their son *both* parents beneath the same roof.

'You can't be serious!' Winnie exclaimed, challenging that outrageous announcement that he would not allow her to leave the island.

'You haven't given me a choice,' Eros parried with harsh conviction. 'Do you think I don't appreciate that your grandfather will be standing by waiting for the opportunity to steal you and Teddy back from me?'

Her lashes flickered up on startled eyes and she turned her head away again, the muscles in her slight shoulders rigid with strain. Something else she hadn't thought about, she scolded herself in exasperation: Stam Fotakis would not take defeat lying down. Her grandfather would remain determined to get his own way and he would not be fussy about his methods. But it galled her to see herself and her child at the centre of a tug of war between two powerful men.

'If you somehow contrive to escape and return to Stam, that will be your choice,' Eros delineated in a driven undertone. 'But you will *not* sacrifice *my* son to his care.'

'Oh, drop the drama!' Winnie scoffed. 'My grandfather would not harm a hair on Teddy's head and nothing you can say would convince me otherwise!'

'I only have to look at your family's history to know that Stam has very poor parenting skills and I won't subject my son to that experience.'

'I don't know what you're talking about,' Winnie argued in frustration. 'Grandad cares about Teddy.'

'I *assume* he cared for his own sons at one time, as well,' Eros countered very drily. 'But he still flung your father out to sink or swim for defying him when he was only a teenager. As for your uncle, Nicos, he made the mistake of marrying a woman your grandfather disapproved of. She was a divorcee and Stam refused to even meet her. When your uncle died, your grandfather and he were estranged.'

Winnie dropped her head, her eyes troubled, because she hadn't known that salient fact. Stam had told her only that his elder son had died in an accident, not that father and son had been at daggers drawn at the time of his passing. And rightly or wrongly, it did make her question her innate faith in the older man because evidently her grandfather had made an almighty mess of keeping his own family together.

'And don't kid yourself that Stam would give Teddy any easier a ride if he failed his expectations,' Eros completed grimly.

'Point taken,' Winnie conceded stiffly, wanting the subject dropped because it was patently obvious that Eros knew more about her grandfather than she did.

'And Stam will never accept me. He's too much of a snob,' Eros added grimly. 'In his eyes, I'm nouveau riche…and there're no princess grandmothers in my family tree!'

'That sort of thing isn't important to me,' Winnie muttered uncomfortably.

'Pedigree is *very* important to your grandfather. Don't ever forget that. He wanted a ring on your finger to gloss over the reality that you were an unmarried mother and that's where my role was supposed to end. I was good enough for you to marry but not good enough to be accepted into the Fotakis family.'

'Scarcely matters now,' she mumbled helplessly.

But Eros wasn't listening. He stalked indoors, his long lithe legs powering him towards the bar in the corner of the ballroom. Momentarily released from tension, Winnie allowed herself to breathe again. She congratulated herself on not losing her temper and leant back against the iron balustrade, letting the strain slowly trickle out of her muscles.

Eros strode back, his entire focus locked to Winnie's slight figure. With her luxuriant mane of dark hair shifting in the light breeze below the sparkling diamond tiara and her caramel eyes bright in her heart-shaped face, she looked tiny and gorgeous and that reluctant acknowledgement only unleashed a stronger tide of aggression within him. She had betrayed his trust and she wasn't a fitting mother for a vulnerable child. How *could* she be? In marrying him and as quickly walking out on him again she had demonstrated that she had very few principles, least of all when it came to reliability and honesty.

Winnie didn't really want a drink but she accepted the glass of wine Eros extended because she was thirsty and if he was offering a polite olive branch, she was more than willing to grasp it. Taut as a bowstring, she sipped nervously at the wine.

'When I asked you to marry me, it was the real deal,' Eros intoned with level diction, his lean, darkly handsome features sombre. 'There was no deception involved and no lies. I intended to be a husband to you and a father to my son and I planned to fulfil both roles to the very best of my ability.'

Winnie breathed in so deep she felt dizzy when the cool salty air flooded her lungs. She flung her slim shoulders back, brown eyes bright with anger. 'Don't you dare try to talk down to me when you threatened to harm my sisters by exposing their secrets!'

'That doesn't excuse you for entering that church and speaking vows you had no intention of following through on!' Eros ground out wrathfully. 'That was *wrong*!'

'Your threats were equally wrong.' Winnie fought back with a flush rising in her cheeks. 'I couldn't risk allowing you to humiliate my sisters any more than I could risk losing my son, so don't you *dare* tell me that you were offering me "the real deal" because you didn't give me any options!'

'I chose to do what was best for all three of us and I put Teddy first. You've *never* put him first,' Eros condemned grimly. 'If you had, you wouldn't have kept us apart.'

'Wouldn't I have?' Winnie gasped, so furious that she could hardly breathe for the tightness of the corseting built into her grown and squeezing her ribs. 'You were such a great role model for an innocent little boy, weren't you? A married man having an affair with an employee behind his wife's back? Do you really think you were the kind of father I wanted or needed for my son?'

'Perhaps not but I *was* his father and I had rights,' Eros reminded her without remorse. 'Rights and responsibilities you were happy to ignore and deny.'

Clutching her wine glass, Winnie gave way to her impatience and moved forward to push past him and return indoors. 'We've already been through this argument. There's no point going there again!' she proclaimed.

'I married you in good faith. I didn't even demand a signature on a prenup. *Why?* I was fool enough to trust you.'

Breathless and troubled with her cheeks on fire with mortification, Winnie snatched up the bottle of wine on the bar and refilled her glass. 'More fool you, then!' she shot back at him defiantly, reasoning that as he had already won the most important battle she had little more to lose from aggravating him.

Eros was outraged. Quiet, trusting, naive little Winnie, it seemed, had only ever existed in his own imagination, a romantic fiction more than a reality. 'A fool no more,' he reminded her with dark satisfaction. 'I have my wife and my child in my home where I wanted them to be.'

'And much good may it do you!' Winnie hurled back as she moistened her dry mouth with more wine. 'I am *not* your wife in any way that counts.'

Eros dealt her a sizzling all-male smile of one-upmanship, recalling how his bride had melted in his arms a bare hour before she'd walked out on him. Some things Winnie could fake but not that burning chemistry and in retrospect he recalled the signs of disquiet he had noticed in her and misinterpreted as shyness. To a certain degree she had changed. She had toughened up, learned to challenge him and she refused to hang her head and admit regret. But at heart and in the only field that really mattered, he told himself, she was still *his* Winnie, as red hot for him as he was for her.

That flashing smile made Winnie feel dizzy where she stood and she blinked, her throat convulsing as she acknowledged the strain of trying to defend herself when her own heart and logic also screamed that she had done wrong. Two wrongs would never make a right. Her grandfather's machinations and desire for revenge had tied her up in knots. But she *had* put Teddy first when she'd readily agreed to her son having a proper relationship with his father.

Marriage, however, had been a step too far for her, a much too personal and humiliating step that had cost her the independence and pride she had worked so hard to re-establish since Teddy's birth. Between them, her grandfather and Eros had torn her life apart. Even worse, Eros had hurt her badly once and she wasn't prepared to risk that happening again. Naturally she could be civil to her son's father, but she couldn't treat him as a husband or trust him, not when she was degradingly conscious that he had only married her for Teddy's benefit.

'You married me intending to cheat me of both a marriage and a son,' Eros grated in a tone of raw frustration. 'What is your answer to that?'

Winnie drained her wine and set the empty glass down with a sharp little snap on the bar before turning on her heel and simply walking away from him.

'*Winnie!*' Eros ground out wrathfully.

Winnie paused. 'You know, I always hated my name. My parents shortened it from Winifred to Winnie and now I don't like Winnie either,' she muttered almost conversationally. 'It makes me think of a horse—'

'*Thee mou...*' Eros bit out, his strong jaw clenched hard as she turned in a reluctant half circle to look at him again. 'What nonsense are you speaking?'

'I've got nothing more to say to you.' With

extreme unwillingness, Winnie focused on him again. Eros Nevrakis, her husband, and he was as gorgeous as a lustrous jungle cat, full of energy and predatory drive. He was judging her as she had once judged him because she had lied by omission in agreeing to marry him when she'd had no intention of staying married to him or even of living with him. He had found her out when he'd caught her in the act of leaving him and there was no coming back from a sin that barefaced.

'I have plenty to say to you.'

Halfway up the sweeping staircase, Winnie stilled and turned back. 'Really? That must feel very much out of character. A little more than two years ago when it mattered, you had nothing to say to me.'

His stunning bone structure snapped taut, stormy green eyes narrowing with wariness. 'You vanished. You didn't give me the chance to say anything.'

'Be honest for once,' Winnie challenged. 'You had nothing of any value to say to me back then. I was just a fling for you.'

Eros gritted his even white teeth. 'We've got enough trouble in the present without digging back into the past!' he derided without hesitation.

'But that past formed the present and my opinion of you and, no matter how hard I try to be civilised and gracious and consider Teddy, I can't get over the fact that I hate you more than any man alive!' Winnie flung truthfully.

As Winnie raced on up the stairs, Eros froze where he stood, colour ebbing from below his bronzed complexion. She didn't *hate* him, she told herself fiercely; she refused to accept that. Why the hell had she brought up the past? That past was better left buried and untouched. He couldn't go back and change anything about it. He had been married... *fact*. He had let her down when she had most needed him... *fact*.

As Winnie pushed through door after door in vain search of her luggage, she finally arrived in front of the double doors at the end of the corridor and thrust the doors wide. Her single suitcase filled with old garments she had been content to leave behind sat still packed by the wall.

Eros leant back against the doors to send them slamming shut. He watched her twist to try to reach the buttons at the back of the gown, the same buttons he had planned to undo one by one as he stripped her bare. His mouth ran dry, the throb at his groin a provocative reminder of his susceptibility to a woman he could not trust. The reaction infuriated him.

'You lied to me,' he condemned.

Winnie spun round, her face aflame. 'I didn't lie. I went through with the wedding.'

'You think that's enough to excuse you?' he derided.

'No, but it's the best you're going to hear.'

'You don't hate me,' he told her, stalking with fluid, boneless grace across the wooden floor that separated them. 'A woman doesn't kiss a man the way you kiss me when she hates him.'

Winnie tossed her head, lustrous strands of mahogany hair tumbling round her hot face. 'That's just sex,' she told him dismissively. 'It doesn't have anything to do with emotions. I believe *you* taught me that.'

Taut with arousal, Eros surveyed her in frustration and reached for her. 'Let me undo those buttons for you.'

'They're hooks underneath, not buttons,' she muttered breathlessly, as if she was making a very important point. Eros turned her round, long, lean fingers gentle but firm on her slight shoulders. With just that single touch her treacherous body ran from zero to fifty in awareness and she stiffened, disturbingly conscious of the hooks giving way at her spine and the smooth brush of his fingers across sensitive skin.

'I can't be that way again with you... I just can't!' she exclaimed in sheer desperation, all too conscious of the melting heat blossoming low in her pelvis, the licking temptation ready and willing to drag her down into sensual oblivion. She supposed that was natural. Eros had taught her to crave him and she had suppressed that side of her nature ever since, refusing to acknowledge it, afraid of falling victim to that weakness again.

Lean hands heavy on her shoulders, Eros nudged her hair out of his path and pressed his mouth passionately to the soft skin at her nape, sending a darting tingle of shivering lust down her taut spinal cord. 'I haven't been with any woman since I was last with you,' he admitted in a charged undertone.

Still quivering from the wickedly provocative assault of his hungry mouth on her skin, Winnie went rigid at those words and then suddenly tore herself free to spin round and look up at him in frank disbelief. 'I don't believe you,' she told him boldly.

Stormy green eyes pierced hers in unashamed challenge. 'Whether you accept it or not, it happens to be the truth.'

Oxygen bubbled in the back of her throat, scrambling her breathing as she gazed up at him in bewilderment. 'But *why*? I mean, you were divorced… Why wouldn't you have found someone else?'

His proud bone structure pulled taut, his exotic cheekbones prominent, the shadowy hollows beneath adding stark definition. 'I've never been into casual encounters and I didn't want to rush into anything either. I won't let sex control me or push me in the wrong direction again.'

Her lashes fluttered, bemusement claiming her. She was barely breathing as she listened because he had never told her that much before and, ironically, he both gave to her and then took away again with those words. First, he implied that what he had shared with her had *not* been casual and then he suggested that sexual desire had once got him involved with the wrong woman. Did he mean her or his ex-wife? Or some other woman from his past?

What did strike her almost dumb was that Eros, for all his gorgeous vital masculinity and electrifying sexuality, had almost as many quirks, inhibitions and fears as she had. Nothing had ever shaken her as much as that revelation because it simply transformed her view of him, turning him from the ruthless, dishonest sexual predator she had believed him to be into a much more human male with his own secrets and vulnerabilities.

Winnie stared up at him, her heart-shaped face solemn. 'You're telling me the truth, aren't you?'

An ebony brow quirked. 'Why would I lie about something like that? What man boasts about celibacy in this day and age?'

Winnie closed her eyes because of the scratchy sting prickling at the backs of them, fighting off the threat of tears. Her feathery lashes drifted down onto her cheeks to conceal her expression. With a husky groan, he hauled her into his arms. Passionate urgency sprang from every line and angle of the lean, fit body pressed hard against hers. His hungry mouth crushed hers, his tongue sliding between her lips to delve deep until a shudder racked her slight frame.

'I don't want to rip the dress,' Eros muttered roughly, spinning her round in front of him and addressing his attention to the many buttons still to be undone.

'Why not? I'll never wear it again,' Winnie murmured, already wondering what lay ahead for them now because they were racing fast into unknown territory and, although she knew she ought to step back and demand her own space and resist the intimacy he wanted, she was as still as a statue, her pupils dilated, her body all of a quiver in anticipation of what he would do to her and how that would make her feel.

Eros ran through hook after hook, impatience gripping him in waves, and he too was fighting off second thoughts. He was picturing her as she'd walked down the aisle towards him, reminding himself that that had all been showmanship designed to fool him and lull him into a false sense of security. She had *never* intended to be his wife, *never* intended to share his bed and his fury at that reality that was still dug down deep inside him. What was he playing at? Getting entangled with Winnie again was like playing with fire and it would be all the more dangerous because of her connection to Stam Fotakis, who would destroy him if he could.

He stared down at the subtle line of her smooth back and the violin curve of her shapely hips slowly being exposed, and ferocious need broke through the defensive barriers his brain was trying to resurrect. Suddenly nothing mattered beyond *having* her again. He pushed the parted edges of the bodice apart and watched the wedding dress fall down to her feet in a silky pool of lace. Underneath she wore white lace panties and pale thigh-high stockings and he took his time appreciating that view of feminine perfection.

Slowly he turned her back to face him and then he dropped to his knees in front of her to smooth lean brown hands very slowly up over her beautiful legs until he reached the delicate skin above the lace stocking tops. Winnie went rigid beneath the caress, staring down at him with almost dazed eyes as he gently nudged her slender thighs apart. She could feel every brush of his fingertips across her inner thighs and it set up a chain reaction in her pelvis, awakening a surge of heat that made her squirm.

'There's so much I want to do that I don't know where to begin,' Eros said softly as his hands curled into the edges of her panties and slowly peeled them down.

Winnie literally stopped breathing, fierce colour sweeping up her throat to engulf her face. She had never been more conscious of being bare.

'Am I *still* the only guy to see you like this?' Eros growled as he tugged the undergarment free by dint of delicately lifting each stiletto-heeled foot in turn.

Winnie toyed with the idea of lying out of pride but then her innate practicality squashed that idea. 'When would I have had the time?' she muttered ruefully. 'First I was pregnant and then I had Teddy and then I was struggling to look after him and work unsocial hours.'

Smiling with unashamed satisfaction, Eros leant forward and planted a kiss on her lower belly. 'I'm grateful,' he confided quietly.

Her tummy muscles tensed. Alarmingly conscious of the stretch marks that were slowly fading into silvery lines there, Winnie swallowed hard, wondering if he had noticed, reckoning he was too smooth to comment on her flaws. And, of course, there were flaws, she scolded herself, because a body that had carried a baby changed and there was nothing to do but live with those changes.

Impervious to her insecurities, Eros vaulted upright and scooped her up to settle her down on the wide bed. As he stood over her, he threw off his jacket, jerked loose his grey silk spotted tie and unbuttoned his crisp white dress shirt. All male purpose blazed in the smouldering green eyes welded to her.

'I have never wanted anything so much as I want you at this moment,' he told her rawly, and she recognised the faint hint of anxiety that accompanied that admission as if that level of desire spooked him.

Yet he had always made *her* feel like that, she acknowledged, as though she was especially sexy and necessary to him, as though he truly *needed* her on some deep fundamental level. It was hardly surprising that she had fallen in love with him. But all Eros had ever needed from her was sex, she reminded herself ruefully. Quickly, she shrugged the thought away again, possessed as she was by a powerful need of her own to live in the moment and look neither forward to a dim future nor back to a past that still wounded her.

Eros pulled off his shirt, exposing a bronzed torso straight out of her most feverish feminine fantasy, lean muscle rippling with his every movement to define powerful pectorals and a stomach that was a taut flat study of hard, corrugated sinew. She stared, her hands falling back from the curves she had been trying to cover, the foolishness of such reticence with her child's father sending a tide of self-conscious red up into her cheeks. It was a little late in the day for modesty, she told herself impatiently, particularly when there was nothing modest about what Eros made her feel.

Excitement was already licking up through her like a storm warning, her mouth dry, her heart beating so fast it felt as if it was pounding through her entire body. Eros had always had the ability to make her feel like a very different woman from her quiet and sensible self. He only had to look at her a certain way, touch her a certain way and she was transformed into a wanton creature that wanted, *craved*, needed…

'I have no patience, *moraki mou*,' Eros breathed as he stripped off his trousers, revealing black boxers that he skimmed off with a similar lack of ceremony.

'You never had,' Winnie whispered shakily, striving not to stare at his body, a hot flush surging at the heart of her and a wave of desire she could not suppress.

Eros laughed, assailed by memories he hadn't examined in years, and acknowledged that when it came to her patience had never been his strong suit. Desire had ridden him hard, frustrating his attempt to keep their affair cool and within bounds, demanding more from him than he had ever wanted to give. He shook off the disturbing memories to concentrate on the pale voluptuous vision of loveliness that was Winnie lying across the bed, her wondrous curves exposed for his appreciation.

He came down to her in one lithe movement, all controlled grace and masculine heat, claiming her mouth with demanding, shattering force and for several long moments Winnie was in heaven because nobody could kiss like Eros. Big hands cupped her full breasts, pushing them together to enable him to hungrily tease her straining nipples to lush prominence. Darting arrows of erotic need raced to her core. He worked his sensual path down over her writhing length. He made her hot as hell, her hips rising involuntarily as he ground down on her, letting her feel the full force of his arousal against the most tender spot on her entire body.

'*Thee mou...* You drive me insane,' Eros husked, his hands lifting to pinch at her already swollen and sensitive nipples, wrenching a long, sobbing breath from her parted lips as her back arched in helpless response.

He forced her still before tugging her thighs apart and burying his mouth there to feast on her sensitive flesh with a passionate carnality that made her jerk and moan. Long fingers traced her tender folds and glided between, probing her honeyed depths with precision while his thumb delicately strummed against her, and then he employed his tongue. She shook and gasped as the slow tormenting rise of an explosive climax ached unbearably in her pelvis.

Eros watched her rise beneath him with a breathless little scream at the intensity of the pleasure flooding her, and then fall back, limp and drained against the tumbled pillows. The look of bliss on her face sent a zinging throb of lust straight to his groin, leaving him hard as steel.

'Let me touch you,' she mumbled breathlessly as he lifted back from her and she sat up, taking him by surprise as she tugged him back down onto the bed beside her. 'I have my own agenda.'

'You...*do*?' Eros prompted, taken aback by her sudden boldness for she had always been a shy lover, content to let him take charge.

Winnie nodded feverishly, her heart-shaped face a curious study of self-consciousness and determination. Her small hands spread across his pectoral muscles and then slowly traced down over his tautly muscled stomach, feeling him flex and tense beneath her ministrations even while she recognised his surprise in some dismay.

In the past with Eros, she had been passive, far too afraid of making a clumsy wrong move and either making him laugh or turning him off. But the news that there had not been another woman in his bed since he had last been with her had thrilled Winnie as much as it had startled her and now all the fantasies she had once suppressed, all the desires she had been afraid to express, were powering her. A little voice in the back of her head was also reminding her that Eros could hardly keep his hands off her and that it was past time that she was woman enough to explore her own hunger for him.

She lowered her head, mahogany hair trailing softly across his stomach as she traced the little furrow of dark hair usually visible above his waistband with the tip of her tongue. As she simultaneously stroked his long, thick, urgent length with her hand, his hips lifted and she heard his breathing hitch in surprise. He was so smooth and hard and warm and, as she soon learned, incredibly responsive to her smallest touch. His hand dug into her thick hair and he arched up to her with an uninhibited moan of pleasure as she laved him with her tongue. For the first time ever with Eros, Winnie felt truly powerful and sexy.

He withstood her attentions for only a few moments before he dragged her back up to him with a kind of wildness that excited her and rasped, 'I can't take any more of that. I want to come inside you…'

Flushed and breathless, Winnie grinned at him. 'To be continued, then,' she mumbled.

With a wildly impatient hand, Eros grabbed protection from beside the bed and yanked her slight body under him with decisive force. Delighted giggles at his unashamed urgency tumbled from Winnie's lips. Crushing her reddened mouth beneath his, he extracted a hungry kiss of retribution.

'Silence, *mikri magissa mou*,' Eros urged roughly as he pushed back her thighs with hard hands.

Mikri magissa mou... My little witch. Winnie savoured the label with pleasure, satisfied that her more daring approach had passed muster.

Almost at the same moment, Eros plunged with a savage growl of satisfaction between her thighs and the ability to think clearly was stolen from her. Her body lurched and shivered with the sweet piercing delight of giving way to his, sensations that she had forced herself to forget racking her with waves of delirious pleasure. Every stroke set her on fire, her excitement climbing with every slick move of his hips as he picked up speed, and then there was nothing but the breathless surging exhilaration of his dominance pushing her to the summit again. Heart racing, body writhing, she burned up in the fiery blaze of release that consumed her from the inside out. Electrifying ripples of excitement convulsed her and held her suspended until she tumbled back in a daze to the real world again.

Eros freed her from his weight and then pulled her into his arms, which startled her because once

Eros had been chary of touching her after sex, his innate reserve kicking in immediately afterwards, making her drown in discomfiture at a moment when she had craved something less ephemeral than physical satisfaction. Now he took the time to stroke her damp hair back from her brow, gazing down at her with glittering emerald-green eyes while he traced the voluptuous line of her lower lip with a thoughtful fingertip.

'I'd like to ditch the protection and have another child,' he admitted huskily, disconcerting her even more with that confession. 'I missed out on all that the first time around and I'd enjoy the chance to experience it with you.'

'Are you insane?' Winnie was startled enough to demand before she could even consider the meaning of such an unexpected proposition. 'Teddy is only eighteen months old. We don't even know if we *have* a future together.'

'I might trust you a little more if I could see you *commit* to that future with me by conceiving another child,' Eros confessed with measured cool. 'The future is there for us to grab and we've got nothing to lose by going for it straight away and ignoring your grandfather's feelings about us staying married. Of course, if you *prefer* to keep your options open…'

'I'm not ready to have another child yet,' Winnie muttered flatly, still struggling to master her shock at such a suggestion from him. 'Particularly not with a man who once chose not to tell me that he was married and who broke my heart. You may not trust me but *I* don't trust you either! Only couples who are happy and secure together should bring babies into the world.'

At that unhesitating rejection, dark colour sprang up in a feverish line across his high cheekbones, accentuating his shimmering sea-glass eyes. 'We *could* be happy.'

'Could!' Winnie scorned as she snaked free of him and wriggled off the edge of the bed to head into the bathroom, needing space and privacy from him. 'That's not enough!'

His sheer high-voltage sexuality sent her brain careening into the realms of fantasy. But way before that acknowledgement, she had been knocked emotionally sideways by his insistence that he had not slept with another woman since he had last been with her two years earlier. And that had shocked her, but what had shocked her even more was that she had believed him and, rightly or wrongly, it had brought her barriers crashing down, making her vulnerable. It had also encouraged her to do what she had sworn never to do again and that was sleep with Eros. But at the same time, she was currently married to Eros Nevrakis, which *had* to change her outlook.

Or did it? she reasoned frantically. Did being

married to the man she had once loved change anything? According to him, she would be a virtual prisoner on Trilis until he felt that he could trust her again. And when was that likely to be? Particularly when she was not prepared to risk having another child with him. And yet with that suggestion he had ignited the strangest secret yearning inside her. Why? Second time round with Eros, pregnancy would be a very different experience for her because she wouldn't be going it alone as she had been forced to do while carrying Teddy. And wouldn't it be wonderful to have that support and to feel valued while bringing a much-wanted second child into the world?

As soon as she recognised that dangerous thought, she stood on it hard and loathed herself for being so weak, so susceptible to Eros's smallest suggestion. He was asking her to *prove* her commitment to their marriage but *was* she committed? Or simply playing for time while she decided what to do next? And how was he planning to demonstrate *his* commitment? Did he really think that suggesting that she have another child with him was sufficient?

As she vanished into the bathroom, Eros lay there for long minutes, seething with angry exasperation and an unfamiliar sense of rejection. Winnie could be such a plodder, proceeding directly and without deviation from one milestone to the next, no cutting corners, no shortcuts, no risks that could be avoided taken. Their affair had probably been the most dangerous impulse she had ever given way to and it would be a very long time, if ever, before she forgave him for not telling her that he was on paper, at least, a married man. Perhaps it was past time he explained exactly why he had never mentioned it, perhaps she would then begin to accept that the future was what they alone could make or break.

The bathroom door stood ajar and he pressed it back. Fresh from the shower, Winnie was already towelling herself dry, a glorious vision of tumbled dark hair and damp pink sensuality, chocolate-brown eyes anxious as they zeroed in on him.

'Er...*what*?' she muttered awkwardly.

'*Entaxei*... Okay, you win,' Eros breathed tautly, his bone structure rigid. 'I'll tell you about my marriage.'

CHAPTER EIGHT

CLUTCHING HER TOWEL to her full breasts, Winnie froze in astonishment and stared back at Eros. 'But you don't *want* to talk about it…'

Eros shrugged a bare bronzed shoulder. 'I owe you,' he said flatly, striding back into the bedroom to rifle through the drawers in the dressing room.

Having followed him on stiff legs, Winnie sank down uneasily on the foot of the bed, watching while he dragged out a pair of jeans and began to pull them on, lean muscles flexing with his every graceful movement. Colour burned her cheeks and she couldn't think straight for several moments because Eros was knocking her off balance on too many different levels at once.

'You seem shocked that I'm willing to talk about my first marriage,' Eros commented in surprise.

'Even quite recently, you weren't willing to do that,' Winnie pointed out tightly, struggling to get her flailing emotions under control.

Eros sent her a steady look from his stunning green eyes. 'I was too angry then but you're my wife now. You have a right to know certain facts.'

Winnie nodded dumbly, fearful of what was coming next, wanting to know about that marriage and yet in the strangest way reluctant to know, because she was convinced that he was certain to tell her things that would hurt.

'A property developer called Filipe Mantalos gave me my first business loan when the banks wouldn't touch me,' Eros told her, disconcerting her yet again with that opening. 'I believe I mentioned Filipe to you before?'

'Yes, I remember. He helped you out when you were starting up,' she recalled vaguely.

Eros compressed his wide sensual mouth. 'Without Filipe's support and backing I would never have got that first business venture off the ground and into profit. At the time, Felipe was a widower with a daughter he adored called Tasha.'

Unprepared for the sound of that familiar name, Winnie flinched, wondering what else he was about to tell her. Had his first wife, Tasha, also been his mentor's daughter? When he had first mentioned Filipe, Eros had been quite clear about Filipe's role in his life when he was a younger man. For all intents and purposes, Filipe had been the father Eros's own father had been too selfish to be and clearly the relationship had meant a lot to Eros.

'Eight years ago, Filipe developed a brain tumour. He had surgery but the tumour returned and was eventually deemed inoperable,' Eros told her gravely. 'Filipe was always a very practical man. He immediately began sorting out his affairs and working out how best to protect Tasha, who was still a student. He was a wealthy man and he asked me to look after his daughter's inheritance until she was old enough to handle the money herself but, because she was young and vulnerable and very much in love with me, he asked me if I would consider marrying her.'

'Consider…*marrying her*?' Winnie erupted into sudden speech with wide incredulous eyes. 'What age was she, for goodness' sake? Very much in love with you? You were already involved with her?'

'No, prior to our marriage, I had no dealings with Tasha beyond sharing a dinner table with her occasionally in her father's company. She was only seventeen and I haven't dated a teenager since I was one myself,' Eros countered drily. 'I was simply a regular visitor to her home and a close friend of her father's. Without any encouragement from me, Tasha decided that she had fallen in love with me and she convinced Filipe that it was a lasting love while I believed it was only a teenage infatuation. Her father, however, wanted her to be happy and he trusted me to look after her.'

'Naturally, but—'

'He knew I wasn't in love with Tasha but neither was I in love with anyone else. He asked me to marry her and give the relationship a chance,' Eros volunteered grimly. 'He was dying. I couldn't say no to him. Because I wanted him to leave this world in peace, I agreed and a wedding was arranged before Filipe's condition deteriorated.'

'You should've said no if you didn't have feelings for her!' Winnie argued helplessly. 'It was emotional blackmail.'

Eros tensed even more. 'It wasn't like that. I believed that I knew what I was doing. I didn't love Tasha but I *did* care what happened to her. She was a very emotional teenager and I didn't want her to be alone and unprotected as I had once been myself. There are a lot of sharks in the world, particularly if you have money. And Filipe left Tasha *very* well provided for.'

'If she was only seventeen, what age were you?' Winnie pressed.

'Twenty-five.' Eros paced restively across to the windows, his discomfort at the subject he was talking about painfully apparent to her. 'But it was a huge gap. She was a very young seventeen year old because her father had spoiled her and shielded her from real life. I was a very serious twenty five year old because my childhood had been less than idyllic and I knew how hard I would have to work to overcome my father's bad reputation in business. Tasha and I had very little in common.'

Winnie released her pent-up breath in a slow hiss. 'I think you were crazy to marry her. She would've been far too immature for you at that age and if she thought she loved you, marrying her was only encouraging her expectations.'

'I didn't encourage her.' Eros's proud dark head reared up and back and he sent her a reproving glance from glittering green eyes. 'I didn't take her to bed either. In fact, we never had sex.'

Brown eyes locked hard to his lean, darkly handsome features, Winnie stared back at him. *'Never?'* she stressed in wonderment.

'Never,' Eros confirmed. 'Tasha wanted us to have a normal marriage from the start but I disagreed. She wasn't ready for an adult relationship and she deserved a husband who loved her. She also needed to have the freedom her father had denied her to enjoy all the usual youthful experiences. I hurt her pride a lot when I turned her down but I didn't think there was an alternative.'

'So, what happened after that?' Winnie pressed, hanging on his every word, her mind buzzing with conjecture and shock and bewilderment. Whatever she had believed of Eros's marriage, she had always assumed that it was a normal marriage between two people who had, at least, started out loving each other.

'We made an agreement. Tasha wanted to study design and set up her own interiors business. She transferred to a student course in London and I told her that she was free to date anyone she wanted, which she duly did. Unfortunately, however, she couldn't bring herself to extend the same freedom to me. She was too jealous, too possessive to accept the idea of me being with another woman,' he admitted tautly. 'And I *did* promise her that if she still felt the same way about me after she had graduated, I would give our marriage a try.'

'Why on earth would you make a promise like that when you didn't want her in the first place?'

Eros vented a groan. 'Because she was heartbroken that I wouldn't agree to have a normal relationship with her. Although I was convinced that she'd grow out of her infatuation, she refused to accept it. I was trying to let her down gently and allow her to save face. *Thee mou*... I assumed she'd grow out of thinking she loved me!'

'It was still a promise too far. It left your life in limbo,' Winnie pointed out, reckoning that it had been very short-sighted of him to agree to such unequal terms.

A grim look tautened Eros's strong face. 'You have no idea how guilty I felt because I couldn't return her feelings,' he admitted ruefully. 'At one stage, she was crying and threatening to harm herself. I would have said anything, promised almost *anything* to calm her down.'

'Oh…' Winnie swallowed hard, picturing Eros struggling to calm and control a teenage drama queen and wincing in sympathy.

'But you're right. It was the wrong thing to promise because, naturally, both of us were likely to change. But for several years, our unconventional arrangement did work,' Eros told her wryly. 'Just as her father had hoped I was able to watch over her, control her finances and ensure that nobody took advantage of her. We would see each other occasionally for dinner but we never occupied the same house and we lived entirely separate lives. Tasha moved from luxury student accommodation into her own apartment above her first design studio.'

'No wonder you seemed to be single when I met you,' Winnie muttered. 'No wonder there was no sign of a woman in your life. Why didn't you tell me that you were trapped in a marriage that you never wanted?'

'It wouldn't have been fair to Tasha to admit that I felt trapped. She was my wife and I did try to be loyal to her. In fact, I kept my promise to her until I met you because there were no other women before you,' Eros admitted with a twist of his sensual mouth. 'And then with you around suddenly, life became very, very complicated in all sorts of ways. I was married but in my own mind I was still single…and then there was that stupid promise I'd made to her.'

'But presumably she took advantage of the freedom you offered *her*?'

'Of course, she did. In fact at the time I was involved with you, she was actually living with one of her boyfriends. And then *that* broke up very messily and she came running back to me for support, convinced that it was the perfect time for us to try having a normal marriage. That was when you met her, when she turned up at the country house without warning,' he revealed impatiently. 'But by that stage, I knew that I wanted out and that I needed my freedom back. Ultimately she agreed to the divorce.'

'She *is* very beautiful,' Winnie remarked uneasily, an image of Tasha's Scandinavian fairness and endless legs still haunting her. 'Why didn't you want to give her that final chance?'

'Because I felt more like her big brother and when I finally admitted that to her, she realised that that was unlikely to change,' he confessed wryly. 'I didn't tell her about you though. I didn't want to hurt her.'

A dawning awareness of certain unwelcome facts was keeping Winnie quiet and unresponsive. Right from the outset Eros had put Tasha's needs before her own, she concluded unhappily. He had

sent Winnie down to his country house, where
Tasha was less likely to see her or learn about her
existence. He had continually protected Tasha's
feelings and had tried to remain loyal to her in
mind, if not in body. When he had finally gone
for a divorce, Winnie had already disappeared
from his life and even after he had regained his
freedom, he hadn't come looking for her. Those
truths *hurt*. He might not have loved his wife but
she had received a level of caring and loyalty from
him that Winnie had never commanded. In short,
Winnie had only ever been runner-up on Eros's
scale of who was most important to him, at least
until he had discovered that she had given birth
to his son.

As the silence stretched to an uneasy length,
Eros breathed in deep. 'I should have told you the
truth when we first met. I regret keeping quiet but
while I was with you, I was an emotional mess.
Our affair was so intense it unnerved me and the
more I thought about it, the more wrong it felt but
I couldn't make myself walk away.'

'Then it's probably a good thing that I did the
walking away for you,' Winnie pronounced in a
tone of finality.

'Winnie?' Eros prompted with a frown of in-
comprehension.

Stiff with discomfiture at the wounding thoughts
flaying her like knives, Winnie stood up, too hurt

and proud to do anything other than conceal her true feelings. 'Well, I'm glad you've finally told me the whole story,' she muttered hastily as she frantically thought about how best to quickly escape an even more awkward conversation. 'But, you know, all I can think about right now is food.'

'Food?' Eros repeated in astonishment, for he had been bracing himself for questions, comments and further condemnation of the choices he had made.

Winnie forced an apologetic smile to her lips. 'Yes. I'm afraid I didn't eat much today and now I'm starving, so I think I need to raid the kitchen.'

Without further ado, she crossed the room to her suitcase and began to open it in search of something to wear.

Eros frowned at her, perplexed by her mood. He wasn't stupid. He could see that she was annoyed with him and trying to deflect attention from that reality. But did he really want to drag any more of the past into the present? It was their wedding night and it had been preceded by a very long and upsetting day. Maybe, in seeking to avoid further divisive debates and concentrate on practicalities, Winnie had the right idea, he acknowledged uncertainly.

He watched as she dragged a faded silky robe out of the tumbled contents of the case and, dropping the towel, donned the robe in a series of jerky movements. Her heart-shaped face was taut, brown eyes dark and evasive as she walked to the door.

'I bought you a new wardrobe of clothes,' Eros admitted abruptly.

Winnie whirled back round to look at him in surprise. 'Why would you do that?'

'It's a gift,' Eros hastened to assure her.

'How very generous of you,' Winnie responded in a tone that hinted that she thought it rather weird that he should interest himself in what she wore.

But Eros, who found her appealing even in a faded robe that had seen better days, always noticed what she wore because he rarely took his attention off her when she was in his vicinity.

'I don't feel comfortable with you wearing clothes bought by your grandfather,' Eros admitted in blunt addition.

Winnie tensed. 'You're not in competition with Grandad—'

'Of course not, you're my wife,' Eros countered with a possessive edge to his intonation as he studied her.

'All Grandad paid for was my wedding dress. The majority of my own clothes are still in London,' Winnie confided carelessly. 'I don't have summer stuff though, so I can certainly use anything in that line.'

She was *not* going to argue with him, not going to argue with him about *anything*, Winnie told herself urgently. She would get upset, she would be out of control, leaking emotion that would give away too much of what she was truly feeling. And she didn't even know *what* she was feeling, did she?

Hurt. Why did Eros *always* hurt her? Why was she always looking for more from him? What was the point? She had to adjust to the new status quo, and *fast.* She was stuck being married and stuck on an island with a man who neither loved nor trusted her. She still had her son and Eros was terrific in bed. *Count positives,* not *negatives*, she instructed herself fiercely. That was what her sister Zoe would tell her to do…

CHAPTER NINE

'I WANTED TO eat chocolate round the clock,' Winnie admitted ruefully, wondering how Eros could possibly be interested in what her pregnancy had been like but, for all that, he kept on pressing for more information. 'Now, why couldn't I have craved something healthy like salmon or salad while I was pregnant? No, I had to crave chocolate. I put on a good bit of weight.'

'I bet it suited you,' Eros murmured, wishing he had been there for her when it would really have mattered to her and counted in his favour. As she lay in his arms, he ran an appreciative hand over the lush fullness of her breasts cradled in a bikini top. He dipped his fingertips into the cups, skimming the fabric out of his path to expose her breasts and expertly tease the sensitive peaks. 'I *adore* your curves.'

Her mind went blank and she forgot what she was about to say as her spine arched helplessly into the hard, muscular heat of the lean, powerful body holding hers. The tingling rise of heat between her thighs controlled her utterly. 'Someone might see us!' she framed in sudden breathless panic.

'Nobody can see us down here,' Eros replied, turning her across his lap to lower his mouth to the pouting nipples he had bared. 'It's a private beach and we're shielded by the cliffs,' he reminded her thickly while he played with the swollen pink crests until she was gasping and squirming and weak with liquid arousal.

He raked a finger across the taut crotch of her bikini pants. The breath sobbed in her throat as the tender flesh beneath throbbed with pulsing need. How Eros could smash her control that fast when they had made love only a few hours earlier, she had no idea. She only knew that as he began to wrench the bikini pants down and off, she was as impatient as he was. He dipped a finger into her overheated core and she vented a shameless moan, digging her hips into his hard thighs, her whole body ablaze with excitement.

'You're so ready,' Eros growled appreciatively, twisting her round to face him and pushing his shorts down as he lifted her over him and brought her down.

Protection in place, Eros lowered her over him, watching her chocolate eyes widen and the pupils dilate as he entered her hard and fast. And then there wasn't time or space for anything but the wild excitement engulfing them both. He cupped her hips, controlling the pace, rocking up into her when she didn't move fast enough and suddenly all the sensations he induced were tumbling in a feverish, overwhelming surge of power over Winnie and she got lost in them, gasping, moaning, struggling to vocalise the extraordinary strength of the eagerness gripping her. She was straining, climbing, reaching for that ultimate climax and he forced her through the barriers, her body shattering like glass from the inside out, leaving her drained and limp.

Eros responded by lifting her up and flipping her under him instead, continuing the pace in a pagan rhythm. Her heart thundering, her breath catching in her tight throat, she pushed up to him, her body catching fire again as he ground down into her hard and that hint of erotic force convulsed her in fresh spasms of blissful pleasure. His magnificent body shuddered over hers until he finally groaned with uninhibited satisfaction.

But even in that moment, his shrewd brain was working at full tilt. He couldn't keep his wife a semiprisoner for ever, he couldn't *force* her to remain his wife either, but when it came to any reference to the future or that thorny word, commitment, Winnie was maddeningly elusive. He gritted his teeth, wondering if he was destined to live for ever with Stam Fotakis peering critically over his shoulder, ready to whisk Winnie away the instant there was a shaky moment in their marriage.

Both his arms wrapped round her slim, trembling body with innate possessiveness, Eros suppressed a sigh. All marriages had shaky moments, he reckoned ruefully, but he couldn't afford to put a foot wrong. He had to tell Winnie that the island had only become his on their wedding day. He also needed to tell her about her grandfather's threats. But unfortunately, Winnie was already sufficiently wary without him giving her added encouragement to distrust him. And who did he blame for that reality? Eros swallowed a groan, his every past sin and mistake threatening to pile up on top of him all at once.

Winnie held Eros close, her slender length quaking with the aftershocks still pulsing inside her. Her fingers stroked through his damp black curls and brushed against a stubbled jawline on her way to tracing the fullness of his sensual lower lip. As she revelled in that physical closeness a helpless tenderness flashed up through her. For a startling instant, his brilliant sea-glass eyes held hers fast and in that instant everything became so clear to her. She wanted to hold him for ever, she never wanted to let him go again because she loved him, had, it seemed, never *stopped* loving him. She had no idea how she had contrived to deny that fact over the past month. Of course, she hadn't wanted to admit that distinctly humiliating truth even to herself and she couldn't picture ever telling him. That was her secret, not something for sharing even with her sisters.

But, how could she not tell the truth to Vivi and Zoe? She was accustomed to telling them everything and was still on the phone to them most days. She had told them that she was happy but had sensed that they were not convinced. Unfortunately, her sisters had returned to London straight after the wedding. Eros had suggested that she invite them out for a visit but neither Vivi nor Zoe had sufficient annual leave to take another break from their jobs so soon after the wedding.

After all, only four weeks had passed since she'd married Eros, planning to leave him. Since then she had been living on the island with Eros and her son, waking up and falling asleep to the timeless sound of the waves beating the shore below the house. Eros hadn't kept her a prisoner as he had threatened but he hadn't allowed her to go anywhere alone either, citing his concern that her grandfather would try to steal her back by some nefarious means, ignoring her protest that she would not allow the older man to do anything of that nature.

For the first couple of weeks, Eros had taken her and Teddy and their nanny, Agathe, sailing

round the Greek islands. Although the yacht had
been rather more compact than the giant one her
grandfather had borrowed to transport them to
Trilis, it had still carried a full crew and its opulent furnishings and spacious cabins had ensured
they'd enjoyed perfect privacy. The cruise had
been a very relaxing experience, blowing away the
tension of the wedding day that had gone wrong.
And she now owned two fabulous rings. The first,
a magnificent solitaire. *Not* an engagement ring,
Eros had insisted even though he had put it on
that finger. And the second? An eternity ring, a
hoop of sparkling sapphires to mark the birth of
their son.

In Mykonos, they had gone to clubs and danced
into the early hours, and Winnie had been surprised by how much she had enjoyed her first experience of being part of a couple that went out in
public. At the country house, they had had quiet
dinners, nights in rather than nights out. But this
time around, she thought happily, everything was
different and Eros treated her differently, as well.
He was consistently affectionate, both in and out of
bed, tender in private moments and always, always
interested in her and very focused on her comfort
and enjoyment. There had been swimming picnics
in wild, secluded coves where Teddy could run
about naked, long lazy lunches in little tavernas off
the beaten track and more than once she had fallen

into bed tipsy and giggling, having enjoyed herself so much that she'd felt positively guilty about it. They had dodged paparazzi cameras on the beach at Paros and had then been skilfully intercepted by them when they were shopping on Corfu.

When she looked at that tabloid photograph she barely recognised herself because, with her feet pushed into casual leather flip-flops and clothed in a bright red sundress from the wardrobe Eros had bought her, she seemed to have somehow metamorphosed into a more extrovert and less inhibited version of herself. She had a deep tan now and her hair was a tumbling mass of natural waves streaked lighter in places by the sun. She had stopped watching what she ate and was waiting ruefully on the pounds piling back on although the constant activity in and out of the bedroom had to be holding the weight at bay.

Eros was very active, very physical. He had taken her windsurfing and paddleboarding. She swam like a fish and she swam every day. Eros was teaching Teddy to swim and he had hauled them both up every hill on the island to appreciate the views, Teddy sitting on his shoulders or waving his arms in excitement from the confines of a baby backpack. Eros was a great father and he had a hands-on approach to his son that had very much impressed Winnie. Watching Eros with Teddy had convinced her that their son would lose a great deal if he was deprived of his father's daily attention. Teddy was already throwing fewer tantrums. It could be that he was growing out of that phase, but Winnie was also able to see that her son thrived on winning his father's approval and quickly shied away from the kind of behaviour that made Eros frown.

With her, Eros was still the same entertaining and sexy man he had always been, but he was much more considerate and caring with her and ready to talk about anything she wanted to talk about, which was the biggest change she had noticed in him. Indeed, being with Eros and Teddy *made* her happy. And one night a week the staff went home early and Winnie cooked up a storm and they ate on the terrace beneath the stars, which brought back memories of how they had first got to know each other.

But her own contentment and Teddy's didn't mean that Winnie could close her eyes to the necessity of seeing her grandfather and having a straight talk with him. She couldn't just leave matters as they had been when she had decided to return to Eros on her wedding day. Unfortunately, she was very much aware that Eros would not be keen on her going anywhere near the older man.

'I need a shower.' Winnie sighed. She slid off the lounger and pulled on a cover-up before stooping to cram her discarded bikini and other possessions into a beach bag. 'And then it'll be time for lunch and Teddy will be awake.'

'What do you want to do this afternoon?' Eros enquired lazily before adding, 'I could do with getting on with some work—'

'That's fine. I'll have Teddy.' Winnie breathed in deep. 'But I'd like to go and see Grandad tomorrow.'

Eros stopped dead in the middle of the long steep path that led back up to the house. *'No,'* he said with emphasis.

'I wasn't asking for permission,' Winnie warned him. 'Nor am I planning to take our son with me. It would be nice if you could invite Grandad *here* to see Teddy.'

Eros studied her with incredulous green eyes. 'In your dreams!' he grated.

'No, it'll happen. I can't say when because I haven't got a crystal ball but it *will* happen,' Winnie assured him evenly, sliding past him to continue on up the path. 'I'm not going to allow my grandfather or indeed anyone else in my family to be at odds with my husband. I'm going to sort it *all* out.'

'I won't allow it,' Eros growled.

'Not listening…not listening, Eros!' Winnie carolled as she walked steadily on even though she was out of breath from the climb and her cover-up was sticking uncomfortably to her perspiring skin. 'Families shouldn't be divided.'

'And what bush did your mother find you under

after the stork delivered you?' Eros asked cuttingly. 'Families are often divided. My own, for a start.'

'That was a divorce, rather a different situation,' Winnie reasoned. 'But I know it hit you hard as a child when your parents parted.'

'No, what hit me hard was my mother's heartbreak,' Eros sliced in grimly. 'She never got over my father and she couldn't move on. A marriage should mean *more* than a legal obligation.'

'I think it does to most people,' Winnie contended evenly. 'From what you've told me I suspect your father succumbed to a midlife crisis and that sent his life off the rails.'

'I used to see marriage as a sort of sacred trust,' Eros ground out rawly. 'That's why I didn't want to marry Tasha and why I stayed married longer than I should've. I kept hoping the differences between us would magically melt away but I'm not that naive now and I'd be a fool to let you spend time with a man who hates me and wants to destroy our marriage.'

'Well, you see, the point is I'm not *asking* you to "let me" do anything,' Winnie responded with spirit. 'I'm going to Athens even if it means climbing on the ferry and spending hours getting there.'

'And how the hell do I know that you're planning to come back to me?' Eros demanded with suppressed savagery.

'Aside from the fact that Teddy is staying here?'

Refusing to react to the brooding darkness in his lean, strong face, Winnie rolled her eyes. 'Maybe it's time you tried trusting me.'

'Not going to happen,' Eros intoned grimly. 'Last time I trusted you, you said your vows in church and then scuttled off onto that yacht to leave me!'

Winnie went pink with mortification and then suddenly she lifted her head high and tilted her chin in defiance. 'Last time I trusted you, you turned out to be a married man,' she reminded him thinly. 'People in glass houses shouldn't throw stones. We've both made mistakes—'

'This marriage is *not* a mistake,' Eros sliced in, his intonation raw-edged.

'Only time will tell us that,' Winnie parried quietly.

A lean hand enclosed her arm to hold her back as she started up the stairs. 'Then give us that time,' he urged. 'Running off to see Stam Fotakis this soon is like inviting the fox into the chicken coop. He'll cause trouble for us if he can.'

'Grandad only wants what he thinks is best for me, what he thinks is best for all of us. I'm going to tell him about your first marriage,' Winnie told him as she tugged her arm free of his hold and went upstairs.

'You're going to do...*what*?' Eros demanded in shaken disbelief.

'You heard me. I want Grandad to understand that you were in a very unusual situation.'

'What I told you was private,' Eros grated.

'*Please,*' Winnie pressed. 'At the very least he needs to know that your marriage wasn't a regular marriage.'

In an impatient gesture, Eros flung back his dark head, seduced against his will by the softness of those caramel eyes. 'Oh…as you wish!'

'Thanks. Grandad may be stubborn and difficult but I won't cut him out of my life.'

'He cut your father out of his,' Eros reminded her unkindly.

It was a low blow and, from the landing, she flung him an unimpressed look. 'He admitted that that was a mistake but once he'd taken a stance he was too proud to climb down. People change, Eros.'

'You haven't changed in the essentials. You still want to believe the best of everyone,' Eros condemned as he drew level with her. 'It doesn't work. Believe it or not, there are bad people in the world who get a kick out of doing you down and hurting you.'

Winnie thrust wide their bedroom door with angry force. 'You think I don't know that after my experiences in foster care?' she flung back at him in disbelief.

'I don't know. You *won't* talk about those experiences,' he pointed out.

Winnie went very still and then crossed her arms defensively in front of herself. 'In the very first home I went to, my trainers were stolen and I was accused of selling them and lying about it. Vivi was badly bullied by the other girls. In the second I was repeatedly punched by an older boy because I wouldn't give him money. That I didn't *have* any money didn't seem to occur to him because he said I talked too nicely to be poor. The third place, I no longer had my sisters because we'd been separated. The foster father was a wife beater and one night I got in the way of his fists,' she recited emotionlessly, her hands clenching in on themselves. 'After that I was in a state home for a while and by the time I moved back into foster care, I was developing breasts, which was really bad news.'

As she'd talked, Eros had paled. 'Why did you never share all this with me before?'

Winnie compressed her lips. 'People don't want to know about that sort of stuff.'

'But I want to know everything because I care about you,' Eros said levelly. 'So keep talking.'

'If it wasn't men leering at me on the home front, it was adolescent boys. I had several scary experiences as a teenager but I managed to keep myself safe. By the time I got to John and Liz's home, I was viewed as antisocial and difficult. They changed all that. They changed *everything*,' she admitted chokily, tears rolling down her cheeks. 'But do you know why I'm telling you all this? Because I want you to know that family means everything to me and I don't expect perfection. Family can encompass a whole pile of different people. It can be your friends, people like John and Liz, even misguided people like my grandfather, who don't know when to mind their own business.'

Eros crossed the distance between them and hauled her into his arms, desperate to comfort her. He was appalled at what she had gone through without proper support. 'I'm sorry.'

'No, you're not,' she whispered helplessly. 'You're like Grandad. Of course, you don't like each other. You're just sorry you're not getting your own way.'

'Partially,' Eros admitted gruffly, brushing her hair back from her tear-stained face. 'But it's important to me to protect you. I don't want you to get hurt and I'm afraid I don't trust your grandfather not to hurt you.'

'You can't keep me locked up here for ever.'

'Like a princess in a tower?' His charismatic smile curved his sensual lips. 'No…but I'd like to.'

'I know…' Acting on impulse, mesmerised by the stunning jewelled eyes welded to her, Winnie stretched up and covered his mouth with hers. 'But you can't.'

'That doesn't mean I'm giving up.' Eros claimed her parted lips with fiery hunger and drank deep of her response, holding her so close that she could feel every stark line of his big powerful body, including his blatant arousal.

'You can't be…again?' she mumbled weakly. *'Really?'*

'Really,' Eros husked, long fingers lifting the hem of her dress, gliding up to the junction of her thighs to pry them apart and explore, his body already aching for the silken oblivion of hers.

He pushed her back against the wall and hoisted her up against him, the carnal play of his fingers ensuring her readiness. A moment later, he plunged into her and buried himself deep, his breathing raw and ragged in her ears as his hips hammered against hers. It was fast and hard and very erotic, and she shot to a climax so swiftly that she saw stars behind her eyes. Only when her legs slid limply down his hard thighs in the aftermath and they were both panting did she register that he hadn't used a condom.

'You didn't use protection!' she gasped.

Eros blinked, green eyes still dark and sultry with sexual satisfaction. He groaned out loud, raking his tousled black hair from his brow with frustrated fingers. 'I'm sorry.'

'No…no, it's okay… At least, it should be,' Winnie muttered, feverishly calculating dates. 'We should be fine. It's not the right time. I should see a doctor, see about taking the pill.'

'No discussion?' Eros lifted a judgemental black brow.

'Not on that topic…maybe in a year or two if we're still together,' Winnie suggested with characteristic practicality.

'I'm not pushing it. Whatever you decide is okay with me…' he conceded, surprising her. 'And, Winnie? We *will* still be together.'

As Winnie walked into the bathroom, Eros appeared in the doorway. 'I'll head into my Athens office tomorrow and drop you off at your grandfather's estate on the way. But I won't be able to pick you up coming home because I have a meeting in Piraeus and I don't know how long it will run. When you're ready to leave, your security team will arrange it.'

Winnie turned slowly from her beach-flushed reflection in the mirror and gave him a huge smile. 'Thank you,' she said warmly, appreciating the reality that he had listened to her and respected her right to do as she wished even if it went against his own instincts.

'Four security guards to look after me is overkill!' Winnie hissed in disbelief as she saw the men getting out of the car behind to supervise her visit to her grandfather's home. 'Grandad's not about to kidnap me, for goodness' sake. Don't you think that you're taking this security stuff too far?'

'Better safe than sorry,' Eros told her, impervious to reason. 'If they see anything remotely suspicious, they will immediately contact me.'

'And if they contact you, what are you planning to do?' Winnie demanded incredulously. 'Storm the house to extract me in a military assault?'

Eros studied her with a ferocious glitter of emerald fire lighting his stunning eyes. 'I will do whatever it takes to protect my wife and my marriage.'

Winnie groaned out loud. 'This is one of those masculine things, isn't it? A show of strength?'

Eros gave her a flashing, utterly beguiling boyish grin that lit up his lean, dark features. 'It'll annoy the hell out of Stam. I'm warning him politely that I will not tolerate further interference in our marriage. He'll tell you, of course, that I'm paranoid.'

'I don't care,' Winnie whispered softly before she reached for the car door. 'Paranoid or not, you're mine…'

The assurance fell into a sudden silence as she immediately regretted those revealing words and Eros stilled in surprise. 'Am I?'

Far more hers than he had ever been before, Winnie adjusted painfully, her heart-shaped face suffused with mortified colour. She loved him but that didn't mean she had to wave that fact like a big banner in his face. In fact, coolness would be far more effective with Eros. Weren't men supposed to always want what they thought they couldn't have? What came easy was always deemed less valuable.

'I'll see you later,' Winnie framed, climbing hastily out of the car and walking towards the grand front door of her grandfather's home. She had given the older man a brief call the night before to tell him that she was coming to visit. She was hopeful that the month she had been on the island would have given him the chance to calm down and develop a more accepting attitude towards her marriage.

Stam Fotakis was in his office but he immediately rose from behind his desk and ordered his PA to serve coffee.

'I thought you might have taken the morning off,' Winnie remarked wryly as he instructed his PA to hold his calls.

'I *never* take a day off,' Stam informed her with pride, studying her over the top of his reading glasses. 'Unless I'm celebrating, of course, and the fact you've arrived without luggage suggests that I have nothing to celebrate...*yet*.'

Winnie quickly caught his drift and almost winced before deciding to be equally direct. 'I'm not planning to leave Eros. We've decided to stay together,' Winnie admitted, watching the older man's craggy face tighten and darken at that unwelcome news. 'I'm here to ask you to back off and accept our marriage.'

'Thee mou...' Stam Fotakis breathed with a sudden frown of condemnation as he studied her strained and anxious face. 'You're still in love with the bastard!'

His perception made Winnie pale but she stood her ground. 'You have to recognise that Eros and I are a couple and that it is absolutely in Teddy's best interests that we make a go of our marriage.'

'You'd walk through fire for Nevrakis, wouldn't you?' her grandfather breathed in a tone of incredulity as he sprang upright again. 'When will you learn that he is simply *using* you?'

'How is Eros using me?' Winnie pressed levelly. 'I know the best of him and I know the worst of him. Let me tell you about his first marriage.'

Her grandfather raised his hand in an immediate silencing motion. 'I don't want to hear some sob story.'

'It's not a sob story—it's an explanation,' Winnie argued and, as quickly and as simply as she could, she told her grandad about Eros's first marriage.

'Am I supposed to be impressed that I've married you off to a sentimental idiot with silly romantic notions about honour and loyalty?' Stam Fotakis demanded, frowning at her in concern. 'You're making excuses for him, Winnie. He was a married man and he turned you into his mistress!'

'It wasn't like that between us.' Winnie lifted her chin, although it took courage to fly in the face of such opinions. 'And I respect stuff like sentiment and honour and loyalty. I *like* that he didn't blame Tasha or anyone else for the mess he involved us all in. I *like* that I wasn't one of many lovers he took. I *like* that he knows he made mistakes but that he's trying to make up for it now.'

'You do realise that he's not in the same class as a Fotakis?' her grandfather said, frowning with disapproval. 'That in getting to marry you he was punching above his weight? That the very fact that he is now known to be *my* grandson-in-law is likely to make him even richer? And that for an ambitious man, he's done very, very well for himself?'

'Eros is more interested in being a good father to Teddy than in profiting from any association with you,' Winnie told the older man proudly. 'And I'm not a snob. I don't care that he doesn't come from some aristocratic family that have ties stretching back to ancient Greece.'

'But surely it *is* important to you that Nevrakis is honest with you?' Stam prompted, subjecting her to a troubled appraisal and pausing before continuing wryly, 'Well, I'm sorry to disappoint you and damage your faith in Nevrakis, but he *hasn't* been honest with you.'

Stam watched as Winnie turned white before his eyes. He was being cruel to be kind, he told himself soothingly. She had to know the truth, had to accept it. He would keep no more secrets where Winnie was concerned.

As Winnie sipped the coffee she held cradled in one hand, her grip on the saucer had tightened and the cup rattled betrayingly. With great difficulty she held herself still as she stared back at the older man. 'I presume you can prove what you're saying...?' she asked shakily.

Stam breathed in deep. 'Nevrakis agreed to marry you to get his family island back. I scooped Trilis up for a song over thirty years ago when his father went bust and Eros naturally wanted to reclaim it. In recent years he's tried to buy it back on several occasions but I wasn't interested. On the day of your wedding, however, the island of Trilis became his. A little sweetener to the deal, as it were. It cost him nothing,' Stam completed heavily, watching anxiously as her expressive face telegraphed her shock. 'Didn't he mention that bribe? It *was* a bribe. Didn't he admit that he had never in his life before set foot on that island until I agreed to him flying over there to check the place out for the wedding?'

'No...he didn't mention any of that,' Winnie almost whispered, leaning forward to set down the cup and saucer on his desk before she embarrassed herself by dropping it.

'If I hadn't bribed him to marry you, he wouldn't

even have considered giving up his freedom,' her grandfather emphasised. 'And *this* is the man you're willing to sacrifice a splendid future for?'

'What splendid future?' she questioned blankly half under her breath.

'Without Nevrakis, you and Teddy could live here with me and eventually you would meet a man more worthy of your attention.'

'A man you chose, who meets your approval,' Winnie guessed sickly. 'A man who doesn't fight back, a man who allows you to call all the shots.'

'Am I *that* arrogant?' Stam dealt her a reproachful look.

'I don't think you can tolerate or like anyone who defies you,' Winnie muttered ruefully, struggling desperately not to think about what he had just told her about Eros.

She felt as though she had been dropped from a height and had landed on her head, because it was aching and full of chaotic, unhappy thoughts. Eros had married her to regain a stupid island? How did that make sense? Trilis was, admittedly, a beautiful island and Eros had ties there that went back over a hundred years: the little graveyard on the headland contained worn headstones etched with the Nevrakis name. His family had helped to build the church and the little primary school on the steep cobbled street running up out of the village. She had dreamt of Teddy starting school there one day… In a daze, she shook her thumping head in a vain effort to clear it.

'I like you,' the older man reproved her gently. 'And yet you are in your quiet little way every bit as defiant as your father was. I don't want Nevrakis to hurt you again. That is why I told you about the island.'

'I'm afraid I've nothing more to say to you right now,' Winnie said tightly as she rose from her seat, striving not to recall Eros's forecast that her grandfather would hurt her.

Or had it been more of a case of Eros fearing what the older man might choose to *tell* her? A faint shudder of distress and revulsion racked Winnie's slight frame, her eyes prickling a tearful warning and forcing her to blink rapidly. Eros had got an island out of marrying her, a sort of marital buy one, get one free offer. How was she supposed to feel about that? *Of course he hadn't told her.* He wasn't a fool. He was bright enough to know how any woman would feel if she knew a man had had to be bribed into marrying her. Oh, she perfectly understood his silence on the subject, just as she understood the anguished regret flooding her.

Once again, she had walked, blindfolded by love, into a disaster. To make that mistake once with a man was unpleasant, but to make it twice was unforgivable…

'You've only just arrived. You can't leave now,' Stam protested in dismay.

'But you've said what you wanted to say to me. You pushed me into marrying him and now you're trying to push me into leaving him, and I won't be pushed again,' Winnie told him flatly. 'What happens next is my business.'

Only she didn't *know* what would happen next, didn't know what she intended to do with the information she had been given. Beyond confronting Eros, she could see no further, but she paused at the door of the office to look back at her grandfather. 'Whatever happens between Eros and I, I still hope to see you visiting your great-grandson on Trilis some day soon because he shouldn't be affected by adult squabbles.'

'Squabbles?' Stam echoed in disbelief at that insulting term for what he deemed to be a perfectly natural hostility towards the man who had dared to wrong his granddaughter. 'I'll never visit you or Teddy there!'

'That's sad,' Winnie murmured ruefully. 'Family should come first, even if you can't always approve of what they're doing with their lives.'

Winnie walked stiffly back out to the foyer, where her bodyguards awaited her. She was in a daze. Eros had married her to get the island back. Eros had forced her to marry him to *ensure* that he got that island back. Evidently, her grandfather had employed the perfect carrot to tempt. On her own, she hadn't been tempting enough for a man who had already been through one unsatisfactory marriage and would naturally have been chary of locking himself into a second marriage with a woman he might lust after but didn't love.

And that was her situation in a nutshell, she decided sickly while her security team engaged in a series of frantic phone calls to organise a departure that had come much sooner than anyone had expected. Pale as death, she stared at the wall, willing herself to be strong and make decisions. Eros had never loved her and that was unlikely to change. Even for Teddy's sake she couldn't stay in a marriage in which his essential indifference would chip away at her self-esteem every day until she had nothing left.

She was strong, independent, she reminded herself resolutely. She would confront him and deal with the situation without getting overemotional or crying or shouting. Shouting would be pathetic. Shouting would reveal that she had been hurt. She would be cool, *dignified*. As she worked that out, her shoulders eased back, her head lifted higher... and at the same time she would somehow make Eros Nevrakis very, very sorry that he had ever been born...

CHAPTER TEN

EROS SPRANG OUT of the helicopter and took a short-cut across the grass to the house. His lean, darkly handsome features were tense. Winnie had stayed barely half an hour with her grandfather, and after leaving she had ignored his phone calls and his texts. That wasn't like her. Winnie was never petty or moody and it took a lot to rile her. But nothing could silence Eros's conviction that something had gone badly wrong.

Even so, there was no way that he could have persuaded her *not* to visit Stam Fotakis. Winnie might be petite but she could fight like a heavy-weight if anyone tried to drive her in a direction she didn't want. That was why he had let her fly free. He was determined not to make her grand-father a source of contention between them. After all, he wanted Winnie to be happy.

And she *had* been happy before she'd left him earlier that day even if she had been nervous about confronting her grandfather, a man known the world over for his stubborn intransigence. Had the wretched man threatened her in some way? Rage gripped Eros at that suspicion, rage as volatile and blinding as a lightning storm on a dark night. Had he made a major mistake when he'd stood back and allowed her to see Stam again so soon after the debacle of their wedding day? Disappointed by Winnie's decision to stay with her husband and child, the older man must be gnashing his teeth in frustration. Had he taken that dissatisfaction out on Winnie?

Eros strode into the hall, which was curiously empty of staff, and frowned, slowly turning in a half circle.

'You're home…' Winnie commented in an odd, flat voice as she walked out of the spacious lounge. 'Sooner than expected.'

He wheeled round. Winnie was wearing an elegant black knee-length dress, her slim legs and delicate ankles on display. He breathed in deep because she looked superb, the outfit clinging just enough to hint at her spectacular curves. He wouldn't tell her how fantastic she looked because she tended to argue with him when he tried to pay her compliments. But no other word could have better described the tumbling mass of lustrous dark hair bouncing on her slim shoulders and the bright brown eyes sparkling with vivacity above her soft pink mouth.

'I cut short my meetings once I realised you would be back early.'

'Now, why would you have done that?' she questioned suspiciously, although he could not for the life of him imagine anything she had to be suspicious of.

'You stayed a very short time with your grandfather and I was worried that the visit had somehow upset you,' he admitted pointedly.

'It didn't take long for Grandad and I to say all that we had to say to each other,' Winnie told him ominously, staring at him.

It offended her sense of justice that even after a very busy day, Eros still looked spectacular, his charcoal-grey suit smooth and unwrinkled, exquisitely tailored to his lean, powerful body, his shirt white and immaculate, his green silk tie still straight and, yes, that shade exactly picked up the hue of his stunning eyes. Only the breeze outside that had tousled his luxuriant black curls and the dark encroaching shadow of stubble accentuating his beautifully shaped mouth suggested that hours had passed since their last meeting.

Eros quirked a winged ebony brow. 'Anything I should know about?'

'Now, why would you ask me that question?' Winnie asked sweetly. 'Is your conscience bothering you?'

'You're acting very oddly,' Eros remarked drily,

and glanced around in the humming silence. 'Where are the staff? Where's Teddy?'

'I gave the staff the night off and Agathe took Teddy down to the village to have tea with her parents. They asked to meet him,' she told him grudgingly.

'Are you cooking tonight, then?' Eros enquired lazily.

'You'd better hope not. I might be tempted to poison you if I had to feed you,' Winnie told him roundly.

'So, Stam told tales,' Eros gathered without skipping a beat, his intonation as cool as an icicle.

Inflamed by that controlled coolness, Winnie shifted several feet and lifted an opulent gilded china vase from a table.

'Very ugly, isn't it?' Eros commented.

'Not as ugly as the truth of what you did to me,' Winnie countered, studying him with a blazing anger she could no longer hide.

'What did I do?' Eros asked sibilantly, thinking that there was no way that she would throw the vase because she was not the scene-throwing, violent type.

A split second later, Eros learned his mistake as his wife pitched the vase at him with all the force of a shot-putter throwing for a world record. He ducked and she missed, the vase shattering harmlessly against the wall behind him.

'You let my grandfather *bribe* you into marrying me!' Winnie condemned in wrathful disgust.

'No, I didn't,' Eros fielded succinctly.

'He gave you an *island* to marry me!' Winnie flung back at him in shrill disagreement.

'I took the island because he was offering it but that's *not* why I married you,' Eros told her emphatically.

'You accepted this island as a bribe,' Winnie repeated, refusing to listen.

'It would've been foolish not to accept it when I was planning to marry you anyway,' Eros declared, stalking forward as she coiled her hands into fists and made a desperate slashing movement with one of them, frustrated by his self-assurance in the face of her accusation.

A big hand engulfed one of hers in his to hold her fast in front of him and his brilliant green eyes clashed with angry brown. 'The only *truly* important thing that happened the day I first met your grandfather was his revelation that I was the father of a son. Yes, he offered me this island and my family once had a great attachment to this place, but that offer would not have driven me all the way to London to see you, nor would it have made me marry you. It was Teddy who initially motivated me.'

'I don't believe you. You didn't tell me the truth about the island or anything!' Winnie threw back at him tempestuously.

'Of course I didn't,' Eros took the wind out of her sails by replying. 'I was very angry before I married you. I was furious that you had kept my son from me,' he reminded her, retaining his grip on her hand when she tried to snatch it away again. 'But I got over that anger and I didn't want you to distrust me any more than you already did. Telling you about the island within weeks of marrying you would have damaged our relationship and I wasn't prepared to risk that. We had enough difficult ground to cover without borrowing trouble.'

'I refuse to listen to your excuses,' Winnie told him between angrily gritted teeth.

'They're not excuses—they're the reasons why I remained silent. Why shouldn't I have accepted the island when he offered it? My father did ask me to try to reclaim Trilis if I could ever afford to do so. But because I didn't grow up here and wasn't familiar with it, this place didn't mean as much to me as perhaps it should've. Once I saw it for the first time, I felt differently,' he conceded ruefully. 'I felt a connection, although not, admittedly, with this grandiose house.'

Winnie shook her head in a kind of blind panic, terrified of being persuaded out of her belief that she had to leave him to find the happiness she craved. 'I'm going to move out and find somewhere to stay in Athens…so you'll still be able to see plenty of Teddy.'

'I would need to see plenty of you as well for that arrangement to work,' Eros fielded forcefully. 'We can't live in separate houses. I need *both* of you to survive.'

'You have *never* needed me!' Winnie exclaimed, wrenching her hand angrily free of his.

'All that's changed,' Eros countered ruefully, 'is that I no longer fight that need. Two years ago, when you walked out on me, my life suddenly lost all focus.'

'Nonsense, you didn't even miss me!' Winnie argued vehemently.

Eros rested level green eyes on her. 'Of course, I missed you. By the time you left you had contrived to become the centre of my world.'

Winnie frowned at that startling statement. 'I don't believe you.'

'It wasn't supposed to turn out like that. It was supposed to be a casual affair but it was never casual between us,' Eros reasoned with a wry curl to his sculpted mouth. 'I was working eighteen-hour days just so that I could rush down to the country to spend long weekends with you. I was phoning you every day, sometimes more than once. I was behaving like a teenage boy in love for the first time. Often, I walked through the door and within minutes we were in each other's arms. That's *not* a fling. That's *not* a casual relationship. But I was in denial about that because I was still married and I didn't have the courage or the experience to recognise how important a part of my life you had become.'

'I remember you pushing me away.'

'Because sometimes I felt out of control with you and it unnerved me because I wanted you too much for my peace of mind. I tried to tell myself that being with you wasn't harming anyone even though I knew that I was lying to myself. Nevertheless, I still couldn't make myself break off our relationship either,' he admitted in a driven undertone, his beautiful green eyes disturbingly unguarded in their anxious intensity as he studied her. 'The fact that I felt everything for you that Tasha wanted me to feel for *her* only made me feel worse.'

Involuntarily, Winnie was listening. 'Did it?'

'After the divorce when I was still thinking about how I had failed I decided that I was no better than my womanising father,' he said gruffly. 'I had made you unhappy and I had made Tasha unhappy. She was my wife and she loved me and yet I couldn't love her back. I watched my mother go through that with my father when he fell for another woman and I couldn't stand to do that to anyone else. With that on my conscience I didn't feel that I had the right to pursue any personal happiness.'

Winnie stared back at him, disconcerted by the amount of guilt he still bore from the past. 'You should never have agreed to marry her and her father should never have put pressure on you to marry her.'

'And if I did marry her, I should have gone for a divorce the minute she began having relationships with other men,' he added heavily. 'But I'd agreed to that and it wasn't fair to change the rules because they no longer suited me. I tried to keep my promise to her and when I turned to you, I failed, so I didn't make you *any* promises.'

'You didn't,' she agreed ruefully.

'I couldn't admit to myself that I'd fallen for you, I couldn't let myself chase after you when you left either because that would have been admitting that the divorce was all about you. And I couldn't admit that to myself back then,' Eros confided starkly. 'Because that's what my father did to my mother—fell for another woman and went for a divorce. And even though my marriage to Tasha was never a proper marriage, I still couldn't accept that I could have anything in common with a man who was that weak and cruel.'

Winnie was bemused. 'Fallen for me?' she repeated shakily.

'I think I fell for you the first time I met you. You were shy and you smiled at me and my heart felt full and I couldn't take my eyes off you,' Eros confessed gruffly. 'And it was always like that. I couldn't wait to see you when I got home. I couldn't wait to *be* with you.'

Winnie was listening to that avalanche of words tumbling from him with wide, confused eyes. 'You're trying to say you fell in love with me two years ago?' she prompted with a frown.

'Winnie…' Eros gripped both her hands fiercely in his. 'A man who is only interested in clandestine sex doesn't spend hours simply talking to a woman or hanging about the kitchen while she cooks, and he doesn't have to phone her every day so that he knows every little thing she does in her life.'

'Maybe it was a sort of love,' she reasoned reluctantly. 'But it still wasn't enough to overcome your guilt and persuade you to come after me once you were free.'

'I'd have come after you if I'd known you were pregnant. Nothing would have kept me from you!' he swore with fierce intensity. 'But you didn't tell me and I didn't know if you loved me either.'

'Were you blind?' Winnie asked helplessly.

'Winnie, you don't cling or flatter or act like I'm the most important person in your world. You never did. If I'd known you loved me, it would've made a difference because then I would've known that staying away from you was hurting you. But not knowing that, I believed I'd made a big enough mess of your life and that I should leave you in peace.'

'You are so stupid,' Winnie whispered in wonderment. 'And that possibility never crossed my mind…that you could be so stupid and blind about emotional connections. I never wanted perfect. I never expected a perfect man.'

'Just as well. I'm not perfect, never will be,' Eros muttered gruffly. 'But I do love you more than anything else in the world. I was too bitter to recognise that when I married you and then you got to me again.'

'I *got* to you?' Winnie queried.

'Yes, you have a way of doing that. I'm not a naturally cheerful or optimistic person,' Eros volunteered ruefully. 'But being with you makes me happy and of course I appreciated that. The thought of losing you again *terrifies* me, so now you tell me what I have to do to put this right. I can give the island back to your grandfather.'

'You'd *do* that?' She gasped.

'Sooner than lose you? Of course I would,' he admitted bluntly. 'It's a geographical location, it's not my heart, it's not the centre of my life. *But you are.*'

Winnie was beginning to rather enjoy the conversation. She stared up into those troubled emerald eyes of his, reading his sincerity, and slowly she smiled, the tension round her mouth falling away. 'You love me, not just Teddy.'

'Of course, I don't only love Teddy. *Thee mou…* You *gave* me Teddy!' Eros reminded her in reproach. 'Is that what you've been thinking?'

'Yes, I did think that when I married you,' she

confessed unevenly. 'I thought you were only marrying me to gain access to our son. I assumed that's why you were willing to blackmail me into agreeing to marry you.'

'Once I got over that initial anger at having been kept from Teddy, I wanted both of you and I didn't care how I went about achieving that. That's not forgivable, I know,' he conceded tautly. 'But I had a voracious need to get back what we'd had together two years ago and *lost*…and I was determined to let nothing stop me reaching for that.'

Her lashes lifted on reflective eyes. 'What we had then *was* special…wasn't it?' she almost whispered, scared to hope, scared to believe. 'That wasn't just my imagination.'

'Something I never saw or felt with any other woman,' Eros admitted starkly. 'And I wanted it back…you and Teddy both. I've been trying to show you that since our wedding day…that we can be together and happy and building a wonderful future. But not one sign would you give me that you saw our marriage as anything other than a patched-up job likely to fall apart.'

Winnie went pink. 'Another baby was a fairly big ask,' she began.

'And I dropped that,' he reminded her wryly. 'So, what do you want to do about the island now? Shall I give it back?'

'Keep it. It's your family place and we like it

here,' Winnie reasoned with immense practicality. 'It's not as though Grandad wants it back. In fact, he would probably be offended if you tried to return it. I think all we need to do is learn to trust each other again. And we mustn't allow Grandad to influence us.'

'He tried to threaten me into agreeing to marry you. Did he admit that?' Eros demanded in a rueful undertone.

'Threaten you? In what way?' she pressed in consternation.

'He threatened to destroy me in the business world. He could certainly have made doing business more of a challenge by interfering with my suppliers and competing on contracts, but he has enough enemies of his own that I would always have found allies,' Eros declared with assurance. 'His threats were not a serious concern.'

Winnie was shaken at that confession. Stam had been far more ruthless in his methods of achieving his goal than she could ever have guessed. Wanting her to marry Eros, he had attempted to force both of them into doing his bidding and at that moment she recognised that it was time she too disclosed the pressure her grandfather had put on her and her siblings to marry the men of his choice.

'I have something to tell you,' she said awkwardly.

'You can tell me anything,' Eros said encouragingly, settling her down on a comfortable sofa while still gripping her hand, almost as though he was afraid to let go of her even temporarily.

Winnie told him about her foster parents' predicament with their mortgage, which her grandfather now owned. Eros dropped her hand and shot upright, incredulous green eyes glittering. 'He's blackmailing you and your sisters? That's *why* you married me?' he demanded. 'Why the hell didn't you tell me this sooner? I could've stopped him in his tracks and protected all of you by buying John and Liz another house!'

Winnie dealt him a shaken appraisal. 'Well, that wouldn't have worked, not without us coming clean with John and Liz about what we were trying to do on their behalf. And they wouldn't have accepted your generosity *or* ours! John and Liz are much too proud and independent to allow anyone else to settle their financial problems. That's why what we were trying to do to help them had to be behind the scenes and kept secret,' she told him ruefully. 'And that property has been in Liz's family for generations, so moving them to another house wouldn't be the same either.'

'You married me to save the roof over their heads. You married me for a stay of execution on a mortgage that cost your wily old grandfather a ridiculously *small* amount of money!' Eros objected in raw wonderment. 'I don't know whether to compliment you for a selfless act of sacrifice or shout at you for being so naive.'

'No shouting, please,' Winnie muttered heavily. 'My sisters and I had to do *something*. We couldn't just stand by and watch John and Liz lose everything they valued.'

'And it didn't once occur to you that you were marrying a very wealthy man who could have stepped in to offer other options to protect *all* of you from Stam's blackmail?' Eros derided in disbelief.

'No… I would never have been willing to ask you for money,' Winnie asserted ruefully.

'You can ask me for anything,' Eros murmured thickly, settling down beside her again and reaching for her hand. 'No restrictions either. Anything you want is yours.'

Winnie tilted her head back, lustrous mahogany hair tumbling back from her heart-shaped face and her caramel gaze locked to him with all-encompassing warmth. 'All I want out of all this is you.'

'I'm already yours, heart and soul,' Eros asserted hoarsely. 'I have been for a very long time. I'm crazy in love with you. Even the news that you married me to save your foster parents' home doesn't put a dent in my enthusiasm,' he confessed, his mouth quirking at that rueful acknowledgement. 'But then if the sight of you walking out on me on our wedding day didn't cure me of loving you, it looks as though nothing ever will…'

'Amen to that,' Winnie muttered, leaning closer, her heartbeat quickening as the achingly familiar scent of him drenched her.

'I have just two small requests,' Eros breathed thickly, leaning down to brush his sensual lips softly across hers, awareness surging through her body like a rocket to awaken every nerve ending into a sweet ache of anticipation.

'And what are they?' she mumbled in a dizzy haze.

'We admit we love each other every day.'

'Easy… I can do that,' she sighed dreamily. *'And?'*

'We go through another wedding ceremony, one in which you mean every word you say,' Eros instructed, toying with her bottom lip in the most erotic way.

Winnie trembled. 'We can do that too. In fact, it would mean a lot to me,' she confided. 'But if you don't kiss me soon, I might change my mind.'

Eros flicked his tongue between her parted lips. 'I want much more than a kiss, *kardoula mou,*' he husked.

Winnie's slender fingers sank into his black curls to tip him closer. 'And you think I don't?' she teased, buoyant with happiness, every fear laid to rest.

'I don't want to be surprised half-naked by our

nanny,' Eros confided, pulling back from her with a groan at the necessity to bend down and scoop her up into his arms. 'We're going to bed.'

They didn't make it up the stairs all in one go. Eros paused to kiss her and things got a little hot and heavy on the first landing and then they heard their nanny Agathe's measured voice outside and they fled to their bedroom. Later they would get up and be good parents and bathe Teddy and play with him awhile before putting him to bed, but just at that moment, they were both punch-drunk on a wave of love and lust, made all the keener by the knowledge that they could so easily have held on to their pride and lost each other. And in renewing their love, they found fresh confidence and exulted in that intimacy.

Six months later, Winnie smoothed her maternity frock down over the slight bump of her pregnancy. Yes, ultimately Eros had got his way. At least, she had agreed to *try* for another child but she certainly hadn't expected to conceive the very first month and indeed had assumed that it might take the better part of a year. Eros had confessed, however, that he was very motivated to delivering the required result and she had to admit that from the moment she had conceived, no newly expectant mother could possibly have been more spoiled and supported than she had been.

It had been a very busy few months. Eros had bought a house more suited to a toddler's needs in London and they were spending more time there so that Winnie could see her sisters on a regular basis. As they were slowly transforming the house on Trilis into a comfortable and less imposing family home and their main base, it also made sense to have somewhere else to go when the building work on the home front reached crucial stages. Winnie found the island more relaxing and she was forging friendships there. She loved the fact that her son could run wild in their extensive grounds and that the property was large enough for her sisters to join her there whenever they had time off. Eros was travelling less and he had set up a working office in the house.

Two months after they had admitted their love for each other, they had had a wedding blessing ceremony in the little church by the harbour and that had strengthened them as a couple. Saying those vows and meaning them, not to mention her steadily improving grasp of the Greek language, had been a crucial acceptance of their new future together. Eros had insisted that he had only suggested it to benefit from a second wedding night and the apparently unbeatable lure of all those buttons, which were actually hooks. But Winnie, who had been disconcerted by the many little romantic touches her husband had thought up to embellish the occasion—not least the surprise presence of her foster parents, John and Liz—wasn't fooled. He had made that day as special as he made her feel and she could not have been happier.

That very evening they were holding a party in honour of her grandfather's seventy-fifth birthday and he was bringing her sisters with him. Winnie smiled cheerfully. It had taken months for Stam Fotakis to recognise the wisdom of putting away the big guns and making the best of his eldest granddaughter's marriage and family. Eros had had to visit the older man to personally invite him to visit them on the island while Winnie had done her bit in insisting on throwing the birthday party for him. Offered a virtual red carpet, Stam had grasped the opportunity with alacrity and any loss of face involved by that climbdown had been wonderfully soothed by his great-grandson, Teddy, running across the lawn to greet with him with a delighted shout of excitement.

'Your sisters are looking very well,' her grandfather remarked, scanning Vivi in her fuchsia-pink dress, a daring colour for a redhead, but frowning at Zoe, who was practically welded to a seat with its back to the wall. 'Zoe's going to have to get over that shyness.'

'It's not shyness. She just doesn't like crowds,' Winnie said defensively.

'I offered that husband of yours a business

deal and he turned me down,' Stam informed her grimly. 'He doesn't trust me. Said it would put me in the driver's seat if he lost his shirt. He's shrewd. I'm beginning to like that about him. I wouldn't like to see you married to a fool.'

Winnie grinned at that grudging admission but tactfully made no comment. Across the room, Vivi was rifling frantically through a magazine and then passing it to Zoe to read. Curious, Winnie walked over just as Eros appeared and fell into step beside her, Teddy clutching his hand.

'What are you looking at?' she asked Vivi.

'Don't ask,' Vivi advised, white with suppressed anger.

Zoe grimaced. 'The Duke of Mancini has taken over another bank. He must be minted.'

'Let me see…' Winnie grasped the business magazine, ignoring the photo of the very good-looking Italian banker who had destroyed her sister's reputation. 'Have you ever come across him in business?' she asked Eros.

'No, he's rather too rich for my blood.' Eros curled an arm round his wife's back and didn't even raise a brow when Vivi vented a very rude word. 'A member of the Italian elite.'

'Pig!' Vivi pronounced with fierce loathing. 'He's a *pig*!'

'Don't read the article,' Winnie advised softly.

'That's the guy who labelled her a prostitute

in the tabloids, isn't it?' Eros prompted in an undertone as they moved on. 'I remember the name
from the investigation I had done.'

'Yes, that's him and, like a rose in a dung heap,
he is still flourishing against all the odds!' Winnie muttered bitterly.

'I wouldn't take any bets on that continuing,'
Eros murmured as his son wriggled deftly free of
his hold. 'Not with Stam gunning for him. I could
almost, but not quite, feel sorry for the guy.'

'Grandad has never once mentioned his name,'
Winnie protested.

'Stam likes to play his cards close to his chest,'
Eros breathed, striding across the floor of the ballroom to stop his son from clambering up on a chair
to reach the precious birthday cake. He ignored the
screams of protest that followed with the cool of a
practised parent and, surprisingly quickly, Teddy
ditched his fake sobs and started chattering to his
father instead.

Man and child looked so alike with their
matching green eyes and black curls that it always
lifted Winnie's heart to see them together. When
Agathe appeared to reclaim the little boy, Winnie
relaxed more because Teddy was too lively to be
anything other than an accident waiting to happen at an adult party. Some outside exercise and
supper would better suit his needs.

Eros brought her a soft drink while she was out

on the terrace. 'Remember the massive row we had out here on our wedding day?' he prompted.

'I don't want to remember that,' she said truthfully. 'I was feeling so miserably unhappy and angry.'

'You have to go through the bad stuff to get to the good stuff,' Eros told her philosophically. 'My ego was squashed beyond recovery when my bride walked out on me.'

Winnie gazed up into his darkly handsome face, fingers tingling at the prospect of brushing back that silky black hair from his brow, eyes lost in the mesmeric enticement of his, her body slowly humming to life like an engine being switched on. 'If it was, you made a very fast recovery.'

'But then I had you to recover with,' Eros husked, easing her back against the railings to hungrily claim a kiss, groaning as she strained against him. 'You are a witch, *agape mou*. Now I have to stay out here until I'm fit to be seen in company again.'

'I think we can manage that,' Winnie whispered with a wanton little shift of her hips that made his lean, powerful length shudder in response against hers. 'I love you so much, Eros.'

'And for some reason I love you even when you're teasing the hell out of me,' he admitted raggedly.

* * * * *

#3701 A VIRGIN TO REDEEM THE BILLIONAIRE
by Dani Collins

Billionaire Kaine has just given Gisella a shocking ultimatum: use her spotless reputation to save his own or he'll ruin her family for betraying him! But uncovering sweet Gisella's virginity makes Kaine want her for so much more than revenge...

#3702 CONTRACTED FOR THE SPANIARD'S HEIR
by Cathy Williams

Left to care for his orphaned godson, Luca is completely out of his depth! Until he meets bubbly, innocent Ellie. Contracting her to look after the young child is easy—denying their fierce attraction is infinitely more challenging...

#3703 A WEDDING AT THE ITALIAN'S DEMAND
by Kim Lawrence

To claim his orphaned nephew, Ivo needs to convince the child's legal guardian, Flora, to wear his ring. But whisking Flora to Tuscany as his fake fiancée comes with a complication...their undeniable chemistry!

#3704 SEDUCING HIS CONVENIENT INNOCENT
by Rachael Thomas

Lysandros has never stopped wanting Rio! A fake engagement to please his family is the perfect opportunity to uncover why she walked away... But Rio's heartbreaking revelation changes the stakes. Now he wants to give her everything...

Get 4 FREE REWARDS!

We'll send you 2 FREE Books plus 2 FREE Mystery Gifts.

Harlequin Presents® books feature a sensational and sophisticated world of international romance where sinfully tempting heroes ignite passion.

FREE
Value Over
$20

YES! Please send me 2 FREE Harlequin Presents® novels and my 2 FREE gifts (gifts are worth about $10 retail). After receiving them, if I don't wish to receive any more books, I can return the shipping statement marked "cancel." If I don't cancel, I will receive 6 brand-new novels every month and be billed just $4.55 each for the regular-print edition or $5.55 each for the larger-print edition in the U.S., or $5.49 each for the regular-print edition or $5.99 each for the larger-print edition in Canada. That's a savings of at least 11% off the cover price! It's quite a bargain! Shipping and handling is just 50¢ per book in the U.S. and 75¢ per book in Canada.* I understand that accepting the 2 free books and gifts places me under no obligation to buy anything. I can always return a shipment and cancel at any time. The free books and gifts are mine to keep no matter what I decide.

Choose one: ☐ **Harlequin Presents®**
               Regular-Print
               (106/306 HDN GMYX)

             ☐ **Harlequin Presents®**
               Larger-Print
               (176/376 HDN GMYX)

Name (please print)

Address   Apt. #

City   State/Province   Zip/Postal Code

Mail to the **Reader Service:**
IN U.S.A.: P.O. Box 1341, Buffalo, NY 14240-8531
IN CANADA: P.O. Box 603, Fort Erie, Ontario L2A 5X3

Want to try 2 free books from another series! Call 1-800-873-8635 or visit www.ReaderService.com.

---

*Terms and prices subject to change without notice. Prices do not include sales taxes, which will be charged (if applicable) based on your state or country of residence. Canadian residents will be charged applicable taxes. Offer not valid in Quebec. This offer is limited to one order per household. Books received may not be as shown. Not valid for current subscribers to Harlequin Presents books. All orders subject to approval. Credit or debit balances in a customer's account(s) may be offset by any other outstanding balance owed by or to the customer. Please allow 4 to 6 weeks for delivery. Offer available while quantities last.

Your Privacy—The Reader Service is committed to protecting your privacy. Our Privacy Policy is available online at www.ReaderService.com or upon request from the Reader Service. We make a portion of our mailing list available to reputable third parties that offer products we believe may interest you. If you prefer that we not exchange your name with third parties, or if you wish to clarify or modify your communication preferences, please visit us at www.ReaderService.com/consumerschoice or write to us at Reader Service Preference Service, P.O. Box 9062, Buffalo, NY 14240-9062. Include your complete name and address.

HP19R

*Ruthless billionaire Kaine has just given Gisella
a shocking ultimatum: use her spotless reputation to
save his own or he'll ruin her family for betraying him!
But uncovering sweet Gisella's virginity makes
Kaine want her for so much more than revenge...*

*Read on for a sneak preview of
Dani Collins's next story,
A Virgin to Redeem the Billionaire.*

"I went to the auction for an earring. I kissed a man who interested me. I've since realized what a mistake that was."

"It was," Kaine agreed. "A big one." He picked up his drink again, adding in a smooth, lethal tone, "I have half a mind to accept Rohan's latest offer just to punish you."

"Don't," Gisella said through gritted teeth, telling herself she shouldn't be shocked at how vindictive and ruthless he was. She'd already seen him in action.

He smirked. "It's amazing how quickly that little sparkler brings you to heel. I'm starting to think it has a Cold War spy transmitter in it that's still active."

"I'm starting to think this sounds like extortion. Why are you being so heavy-handed?"

"So that you understand all that's at stake as we discuss terms."

She shifted, uncomfortable, and folded her arms. "What exactly are you asking me to do, then?"

"You're adorable. I'm not asking. I'm telling you that, starting now, you're going to portray yourself as my latest and most smitten lover." He savored that pronouncement with a sip of wine that he seemed to roll around on his tongue.

"Oh, so you blackmail women into your bed."

For a moment, he didn't move. Neither did she, fearing she'd gone too far. But did he hear himself? As the silence stretched on, she began to feel hemmed in and trapped. Far too close to him. Suffocated.

"The fact you didn't hear the word *portray* says more about your desires than mine," he mocked softly. He was full out laughing in silence at her. So overbearing.

"I won't be blackmailed into playing pretend, either," she stated. "Why would you even want me to?"

He sobered. "If I'm being accused of trying to cheat investors, I want it known that I wasn't acting alone. I'm firmly in bed with the Barsi family."

"No. We can't let people believe we had anything to do with someone accused of fraud." It had taken three generations of honest business to build Barsi on Fifth into its current, iconic status. Rumors of imitations and deceit could tear it down overnight.

"I can't let my reputation deteriorate while I wait for your cousin to reappear and explain himself," Kaine said in an uncompromising tone. "Especially if that explanation still leaves me looking like the one who orchestrated the fraud. I need to start rebuilding my name. And I want an inside track on your family while I do it, keeping an eye on every move you and your family make, especially as it pertains to my interests. If you really believe your cousin is innocent, you'll want to limit the damage he's caused me. Because I make a terrible enemy."

"I've noticed," she bit out.

"Then we have an agreement."

Don't miss
A Virgin to Redeem the Billionaire
available March 2019 wherever
Harlequin Presents® books and ebooks are sold.

www.Harlequin.com